THE DROWNING BOY

THE
DROWNING
BOY

Susan Terris

DOUBLEDAY & COMPANY, INC.
Garden City, New York

Excerpt from *Charlotte's Web* by E. B. White. Copyright 1952 by E. B. White. Reprinted by permission of Harper & Row, Publishers.

ISBN: 0-385-03981-6 Trade
       0-385-04050-4 Prebound
Library of Congress Catalog Card Number 72–76211
Copyright © 1972 by Susan Terris
All Rights Reserved
Printed in the United States of America
First Edition

For Michael

THE DROWNING BOY

Chapter 1 — Saturday, July 4

"I dare you, Jason," Myra called out.

"Dare you dare you dare you," echoed the limestone walls of the old quarry.

Jason Hurd stood on the swaying tire and stared down at the water far below. The tire was tied to a thick rope which was attached to the branch of an oak tree jutting out over one wall of the quarry. Jason bent his knees and jerked at the rope to increase his momentum. The tire spun in circles. The rope cut into his fingers.

"Jump," Myra urged. "Come on, Jay. You can do it. I'm here to catch you. And Warren's here, too."

Myra Hurd. Warren Price. Myra was Jason's sister. Warren was Myra's newest boyfriend. His blond head was floating on the water a short distance from her brown one. Other people were swimming in the quarry on this hot Fourth of July, but only Jason's sister was treading water directly below the reeling tire.

"Jump down, Jason. Show Warren you can do it."

Jason clung to the rope. It wasn't the height that bothered him. On their farm, he would jump from the loft to the floor of the barn. No, it was something else—something too embarrassing to admit. Jason Hurd, aged twelve, had never learned to swim.

Jason tried to forget his fear. He fixed his eyes on Myra as he spun around, but he was dizzy now and the tire kept swaying in a funny arc. He saw two Myras. Then three—all beckoning for him to plunge into the cold water below.

"Come on, Jason. I dare you."

With Myra everything was a dare—a contest. A contest Jason could never win. Myra was sixteen, and although he was as tall as she, height was not enough. She could do everything better than he could. Like their father, Karl Hurd, Myra had a persistent drive to be the best.

Spinning above the glinting water had a hypnotic effect on Jason. Time seemed to be suspended. He was staring down at Myra, but he was seeing his father's face. Jason hadn't wanted to come to the quarry today. That was his father's idea. Karl Hurd was home because of the holiday. He had been sitting in his usual chair on the shaded front porch of the farm house. With one hand he had been stroking the back of their large muscular schnauzer and with the other holding a can of Diet Cola. Nearby were his barbells, and across his knees lay a .22 rifle.

"Go on to the quarry," his father had insisted. "I'll be along later. And I'd better find you there, not around here monkeying with some god-damned toad."

"Hey, Jason! If you're going to jump, then jump!" Myra's voice was distracting but not nearly as distracting as thoughts about his father.

Karl Hurd was a pathologist at a large St. Louis hospital. One day last summer he had decided that he and his family needed to escape from the city. Then, impulsively, he had bought a run-down forty-acre farm near the town of Viceroy at the western edge of the city. The farm would be a good investment, he was fond of saying, because of the quarry. The long-abandoned quarry was only half a mile from the Hurd farm. It had been flooded to make it the prime attraction for a new housing development called Country Lake Acres. The area around the quarry was already marked with numbered stakes which mapped out the boundaries of the new homesites. Someday, Karl felt, he would be able to sell his farm for a similar development. At the moment, it was a farm only in the loosest sense. There were no domestic animals, no commercial crops. It was forty acres of neglected fields and dense woods.

Most of the time, Jason liked the farm. It was better than their cramped city apartment had been. It gave him enough breathing space to put some distance be-

tween himself and his father. Between himself and
Myra, too. But in the summer the quarry threatened
every day. All the older children around Viceroy swam
there now. All except Jason.

Dizzy, dizzy, dizzy—Jason looked down at the sun
dancing off the water. Myra was still shouting at him,
but he had shut out her voice. He could feel his body
growing limper. Well, he could jump, couldn't he?
What difference would it make anyway? If his father
came jogging up and found him suspended there, his
cut-off jeans still dry, why then Karl Hurd would simply
pry his hands loose and hurl him down into the water.
And it wouldn't be the first time.

Jason didn't even jump, really. He just uncurled his
fingers and leaned back. He lost all sense of space and
time, almost as if he were falling asleep. Then he hit on
the flat of his back with a force that punched the air
from his chest.

He was under the water choking but not struggling.
He lay on his back, and when he tried to breathe his
chest filled up with water.

Myra had him from behind. He could see her sun-
browned arm across his chest as she pulled him up
into the air and light. Jason lay motionless in her
grasp. The strong scissors action of her kick towed
them both toward the nearest limestone ledge. "I've
got him—got him, Warren. But you'll have to help me
pull him out."

Jason was limp as Warren and Myra hauled him up

out of the water. His eyes were closed. He wanted to cough, but he didn't. Instead, he tried to swallow it all down. The powdery limestone felt warm under his back.

With an expert's touch, Myra held his nostrils together and blew into his mouth. She forced her breath into his aching chest. Then, at last, he coughed freely. Coughing and choking, he pushed her back from him.

"Get off me," he sputtered. "Leave me alone."

Myra tugged at the bottom of her swimsuit. Then she wiped off her mouth impatiently. "Oh, Jason, Jason! I said *jump*—not *drown*. You didn't even try, did you? You never try. What's wrong with you? I said I'd help, but I didn't think I'd have to save you from drowning. You are too much!"

Warren was kneeling near Jason's feet. "Are you all right, kid?" he asked. "Are you sure he's all right, Myra? Why didn't you tell me he couldn't swim? Why did we bring him along in the first place?"

Myra sighed. "Oh, I don't know. I always start feeling sorry for him, and then I start thinking I can help him. Anyway, it was your idea. You told Dad he was welcome to come with us."

Myra. This was all her fault, Jason decided. She had meant to humiliate him in front of Warren. It was some kind of plan to discredit him before Warren really began to like him. She was subtle and devious. She always worked this way—cutting him off, leaving him alone. He hated her. He really hated her.

"What's your father going to say when he hears about this?" Warren asked.

Myra shook her head. "Don't worry. Jay always does crazy things like that. Dad says it's because he's left-handed."

"Oh, come on," Warren protested.

"Well, it's just a joke. A family joke." She took one foot and pressed it down on Jason's bare stomach, causing him to spring forward. "See?" she said. "He's all right. He's just feeling embarrassed. Now, come on. Let's swim."

Slowly, Jason pulled himself to his feet. He stood staring at her. It infuriated him that she talked to Warren as if he wasn't even there. But Myra looked right past him. Although he was already dripping wet, Jason could feel himself perspiring in his palms and behind his knees.

Then he said it. Just one word. "Bitch!"

Lunging forward, he pushed hard at her chest with both hands. He wanted to hurt her. The force of his shove drove her backward into the flooded quarry. Then, avoiding the startled look in Warren's eyes, he scrambled up the limestone cliff and ran off toward the farm.

He didn't have to stay around to see if Myra was all right. Myra was always all right. She had arranged things skillfully, and Jason had obliged by making a fool of himself. Now, in private, she could finish telling

Warren all about him. *He doesn't have any friends. He plays with slimy creatures from the woods. One minute he's quiet and the next he's acting crazy. He couldn't fit in at Viceroy Junior High so Daddy had to send him to Hawthorne. You know Hawthorne—right over the hill on the other side of the quarry. That's right. That's the school for problem boys.* And Warren, like the rest, would believe every word she said.

Jason hurried along the dirt path at the top of the quarry and plunged into the woods. Another day he might have stopped at the pond to catch crayfish, but today he didn't feel like it.

He knew exactly what he wanted to do. He'd sneak into the barn and climb up in the loft with Templeton. Templeton was his tame rat, named after the wild one in *Charlotte's Web.* There in the loft Jason could forget about Myra, about Warren, about the quarry.

"Oh, Jason . . . is that you?" His mother was standing in the vegetable garden between the house and the barn. She was tending her young tomato plants. Carefully she tied each one to its own wooden stake. She was different now that they lived in the country. Sometimes she hardly heard what people said to her. When the Hurds moved, she had given up her career as a chemist in a laboratory at the University. She used to grow molds. And she had worked with some kind of acid solution that burned holes in her lab coat. Now she just stayed on the farm and looked after her mother, Jason's grandmother. Instead of growing molds, she grew tomatoes, corn, and geraniums.

After only eleven months on the farm, she seemed years older. Jason looked at her bony frame, covered loosely with the ragged lab coat that hung to her ankles. On her feet, unlaced, were a pair of Jason's old sneakers.

"My tomatoes. . . ." Ellen Hurd gestured hopelessly. "Your father burned some trash, and the smoke has wilted them. Now I must give them extra water and . . ." Her voice faded as though she were speaking to herself. Then she looked up again. "I see you've been swimming. Your father will be pleased. Did you go with Myra?"

There was a crunching sound on the limestone gravel of the driveway. Steady and brisk, the footsteps approached. Crepe-soled walking shoes. "Well, son, are you back already?" Karl Hurd called. "I was just on my way to join you. I thought you were going to wait for me over there."

Jason stared up at his father. For a moment, he found himself gasping for breath, as if he were back at the quarry under water.

He turned toward his mother, but she wasn't listening. She was nursing her wilted plants.

"I've been in the water already," he muttered. "You said to and I did. Now I've come back."

"To do what?"

Jason dug his nails into his palms. "To play in the loft," he said.

"With that god-damned rat? Is that what you're going to do all summer? Play with rats and toads and whatever else you keep stowed away up there?"

In the city, Karl Hurd had felt that the rat made an acceptable pet. But now he couldn't understand why Jason chose to play with a rat, ignoring Nimbus. Nimbus had been Karl's present for Jason when they moved to the farm. He was a big gray schnauzer. Karl had never dreamed that his son would continue to love the rat, that he would still walk around with it perched on his shoulder.

Jason watched as his father's balding head grew red with anger. "If you played with the *dog*, I wouldn't mind. Look at him. He needs exercise, brushing, training. You ought to have plenty of time this summer. Why don't you work with him? Just try it. And Myra —Myra might give you some help, too."

Myra. Myra. Jason didn't want to hear her name. He didn't want to swim in the quarry. He didn't want to train Nimbus. And he didn't want to stand and look at his father any longer. He wanted to lunge out at him. Push him as he had pushed Myra. But he didn't.

For one last instant, Jason continued to stare at his father. Then he streaked past Karl and into the barn. Quickly, he scrambled up into the loft, pulling the wooden ladder up behind him.

Karl Hurd was shouting, but Jason didn't listen. It

was cool and quiet in the loft. He was safe. Besides Templeton, Jason had a few other animals up there—some crayfish, a snake, and two newts. In the loft he kept an assortment of old cartons and dishpans outfitted as terrariums for the woodland creatures he was studying.

Jason unlatched the door of Templeton's cage. Then, taking a deep breath, he peered out the tiny dirt-speckled window of the loft. There was his father, still angry, still calling out after him. And behind his father was his mother, dreaming quietly among her tomato vines. She looked almost like a scarecrow—slow and inanimate in her own field.

"The tail is the worst part," Myra said. "If it weren't for the tail, I wouldn't mind it as much."

Jason stood on the front porch of the farm house with Templeton perched on his shoulder.

"Oh, a tail is just a tail," Karl Hurd said. "It's not that—it's those bony pink feet and that sneaky manner. Sorry, Jason, I wish I didn't feel that way, but I do."

Jason hooked one leg over the railing of the porch, grasping Templeton between his hands. The little creature wiggled its nose. That wasn't sneaky, was it? But the rat was nervous. Its black and white chest was throbbing. Templeton was always nervous when Nimbus was around. That was why Jason had had to move the rat and the other animals up into the loft. Nimbus was always prowling around, stalking the pets Jason kept in the barn.

Right now Nimbus lay asleep in the sun. But even

asleep he seemed to be all taut muscle, like some sort of jungle beast.

Myra slipped down off the porch and knelt by the dog. "Oh, Nimbus," she crooned, stroking his face with both hands, "wake up, you sleepy thing. You are such a good dog, you are. You want someone to play with you, do you?"

Karl smiled approvingly. Then, with a flicker of his eyelids, he sent a brief glance in Jason's direction.

Karl had been lifting his barbells, a hobby he pursued in an attempt to keep himself trim despite the sedentary days spent in the pathology lab. With controlled strength, he placed the barbells back under his chair and picked up his rifle. He squinted past Jason at a row of Diet Cola cans set up on top of the split-rail fence by the driveway.

"Come on, Myra," he suggested, "I'll exercise Nimbus later. How about some target practice?"

"No, I don't think so," Myra said. "I'm supposed to meet Warren over at the stables at eleven-thirty."

"You've got time—over half an hour if we get right to it. . . ."

"Well, okay then. If it's just one match," Myra agreed. "How can I turn down a chance to beat you?"

"Those are fighting words, girl. But just to show my heart's in the right place, I'll still spot you four cans. Jason, what about you? I'll spot you an extra six. All right?"

No, it wasn't all right. Jason hated guns, even when they were only used for shooting at cans. The marksmanship gained shooting at cans prepared his father for killing the rabbits and squirrels that got into his wife's garden.

Jason had never refused outright to learn to shoot the rifle. Instead, he had stubbornly resisted learning to do it well. He seldom bothered to take aim. It pleased him enormously that his father thought he was merely incompetent. Then, too, the .22, with its right-handed bolt, was awkward for left-handed Jason to manipulate.

Like the schnauzer, the rifle was new to Karl. Its purchase also coincided with the move to the Viceroy farm. It was part of a new image, Jason suspected.

Templeton was now nestling inside Jason's tee-shirt, trembling as he clung to the shirt. Nimbus had come up on the porch. The dog stood at attention, growling, his haunches quivering slightly. "I'll shoot," Jason agreed, backing away from the dog, "as soon as I put Templeton away."

"Templeton, Templeton," his father muttered, taking careful aim. "Well, keep him out of my range. You wouldn't want me to hit him by mistake."

"Hurry, will you?" Myra called after Jason. "I really don't have much time."

Jason didn't hurry. He climbed slowly up the ladder to the loft. Templeton could climb that ladder by himself, jumping lightly from rung to rung. Jason had taught him that. But today, Jason carried him on his shoulder because Nimbus had followed them into the barn. Nimbus stood poised at the foot of the ladder as Jason climbed up.

He could hear the first shots of the match as he opened the cage and let Templeton jump back inside. "A cage is an awful thing," Jason murmured to himself. "Why are you always so glad to get back?"

"Hurry up, son," Karl called out. "It's your turn."

Jason latched the cage securely and jumped down out of the loft. As he left the barn, he was startled to see that the barrel of the rifle was pointing not at the fence but at him. Well, not really at him—higher. His father jerked at the trigger, and the shot zinged over his head into the trees. Karl groaned. "Missed that damn squirrel. When you came through the barn door you distracted me. Well, now that you're there, set up the rest of those cans, will you?"

Jason set up the cans and took his turn with the gun. It wasn't much of a contest. Jason did hit a few cans. He had to every once in a while so no one would get suspicious. Karl Hurd won. He always won. He hit 25 out of 30. Myra hit 17. Jason hit 5.

"That was fun, Dad. Thanks," Myra said. "I was going to ride over on my bike, but now I'm so late that I think I'd better borrow Mom's car. Okay? Then I can stop for a few groceries on the way home, too."

"Sure, honey, run along and have a good time. The keys are in the car."

In silence Jason and his father watched as Myra backed the car out of the barn and drove it off in the direction of the stables. After a few moments Karl turned to Jason. "You know, I should buy you a weapon with a left-handed bolt. Winchester makes one, I think. You'd do much better. Would you like that?"

"Maybe."

"All right. I'll see what I can do about it." Karl paused thoughtfully. "Well, what are you planning to do now? Want to come to the quarry with me later this afternoon?"

"No."

Karl looked around. "Say, where's your mother this morning? Sometimes I wish . . . oh, never mind. Where is she?"

Jason shrugged. He glanced toward the vegetable garden, but she wasn't there. She was probably in her room lying down for a nap. Or maybe she was with Gammer. "Don't know," Jason answered absently, staring off in the direction of the woods.

"Well, how about cleaning the rifle for me?" Karl asked.

"Sure," Jason replied. He went to the kitchen for the ramrod, the oil, and the rags. He didn't mind cleaning the gun. As a matter of fact, it gave him a certain pleasure to empty the chamber, clean out the lead filings with the ramrod, and wipe his father's fingerprints off the stock and the bolt.

"Don't get oil on the wood," his father cautioned. "Oil will rot it."

Jason stiffened. That must have been the millionth time his father had issued the same warning. Karl made such a big deal out of everything. He liked to call the .22 a "weapon" because that was the proper army term. What a laugh! Some soldier his father had been. He'd spent his army years in South Carolina teaching jungle sanitation to new recruits.

Jason emptied the remaining cartridges out of the gun. His father sat taking gulps out of a can of Diet Cola. There was something on his mind. Jason knew that. His father never sat still for very long without a reason.

Jason worked on in silence. He was vaguely conscious of Nimbus growling in the garden. Probably after a mole or a groundhog. Nimbus was aggressive but not too smart. He never seemed to catch anything.

At last, Karl Hurd cleared his throat. "Well, son, I've been wondering about your summer plans. What are they?"

Jason frowned. He hadn't made plans. He just wanted to spend time in the woods. "Nothing, I guess."

"Well, I have a kind of idea I've cooked up—a job for you, helping Mr. Slavin over at Hawthorne."

Jason looked up in surprise. Mr. Slavin was the English teacher at Hawthorne. He and his wife had agreed to be the summer caretakers this year. But Mr. Slavin was no particular friend of Jason's. Although Jason was good in subjects like science and history and math, he had always managed to do poorly in English.

"Wandering attention, erratic performance, no sense of commitment" were a few of the phrases Mr. Slavin had used on Jason's end-of-term commentary.

"You'll learn carpentry, son. Sam Slavin is a master carpenter. That's what he taught with the Peace Corps before he came to Hawthorne last year. And there will be painting, gardening, and other odd jobs, too." Karl paused meaningfully. "After our disagreement yesterday, I suddenly saw that you needed something useful to do, so I arranged it with Mr. Slavin. I even called your headmaster at his summer place on the Cape to see if we could get a reduction in next year's tuition in exchange. How about it?"

Jason clenched his fingers around the barrel of the gun. "All right," he agreed, straining to control his feelings, "if you want me to. . . ."

Karl was exasperated by this reply. "If *I* want you to? What about *you?* After all the phoning I did, the plans I made? I'm trying to do the right things for you, Jason. But you don't have to if you don't want to. I just think working with Slavin will make a better summer for you. It will be good for you to learn to do things with your hands."

Jason finished wiping off the stock of the gun. Then, without reloading it, he pushed it aside. At last, he said, "Okay, I'll do it."

"Perfect! Slavin said he'd walk over sometime today so we can work things out. He says it won't make any difference that you're a lefty. I asked if that would make it harder to teach you but he said no. You can do it, Jason, if you'll only give it a fair try."

Jason nodded. His father was concerned; he was making some kind of effort, but Jason couldn't respond. He didn't want to be a carpenter. He didn't want to spend his summer with Mr. Slavin. He'd spent all year at Hawthorne. Couldn't he even have a summer to himself?

"You like Hawthorne, don't you? Better than the junior high? It costs me an arm and a leg, but if it makes you happy, it's worth it."

"It's fine," Jason said. That wasn't a lie. He had been fairly happy at Hawthorne. No one bothered him much. He wasn't ridiculed for being a dreamer. He had been the only day student at the small boarding school, but that had been all right with him. It gave him privacy, time to himself in the barn and in the woods, time he wouldn't have had if he'd been boarding. Then, too, it saved Karl money.

Myra liked to imply that Hawthorne was just for problem boys, but Jason didn't think that was true. A few were problems, but most seemed to be all right. A little lonely maybe—but all right.

Among the lonely ones, Jason had even found a casual friend, a boy named Jimmy Cellini. Jimmy seemed to like Jason. He was interested in Templeton and in Jason's terrariums. At least he said so. Jimmy was fat and he lisped, but he was some kind of genius in math and the best chess player at Hawthorne. He had taught Jason how to play, and they had tried an occasional game during lunch hour. Jason liked chess, but it discouraged him that Jimmy was so much better. Jimmy had gone home to Cincinnati for the summer, but Jason didn't miss him. He'd been looking forward to his second summer on the farm too much to care that he'd have to enjoy it alone.

And then with a few phone calls, Karl Hurd had changed everything. What else was there to say?

While Jason was trying to decide how to put an end to the conversation, his mother drifted out onto the front porch. "Oh, there you are, Jay. I need your help. To take the vacuum up to Gammer's room. It must be cleaned. She's not happy when the room isn't . . ." Ellen turned to glance out at her garden. "Just carry it up and leave it by the door. And see if she wants any water. It's so hot. . . ."

Jason went inside and took the old green vacuum from the downstairs closet. His eyes fastened on his feet, he dragged it across the dining room. Whenever possible he avoided that room because it was dominated by large portraits of Myra and his father. Myra's portrait, done when she was eight, showed her pig-tailed and grinning. The jagged fringe of hair along her forehead was a remnant of the bangs she'd chopped off only a week before. But still she smiled; the world held no terrors for her. On the opposite wall was the picture of Karl, a relic from army days—

painted by a mental patient. He looked somber and intense, his pale blue eyes staring out from under the brim of his captain's hat.

Jason took a deep breath as he made his way up the back steps to Gammer's room. The musty smell of the vacuum prickled his nostrils. Jason hated to go in there. In that room, his senile grandmother sat all day, strapped into her rocking chair. She couldn't walk, and she couldn't talk. As usual, the television set was on, turned up loud for Gammer's aged ears. Ellen Hurd insisted that her mother was still aware of what was going on about her, but Jason doubted it.

From the doorway Jason looked at his grandmother. Her eyes gazed blankly at the television set. He placed himself between Gammer and the flickering picture. Nothing. Gammer stared at him with the same intense preoccupation with which she had stared at the TV. She was shrunken and wrinkled, her body hunched over. On her feet were fluffy white slippers with spotless soles. Gammer seemed to be shriveling up.

Seeing her made Jason feel sad and tight inside. Until three years ago, she had talked with him, cooked for him, walked with him, read to him. She had always looked after him while his mother was working. But after that first stroke, things had never been the same. Now he stood planted before her face and she didn't even see him.

"Not in front of the set . . ." Ellen's voice chided softly. Jason jumped back. He hadn't heard his mother approaching. "Gammer can't see the TV if you block her view. Have you offered her water?"

Jason took hold of a water glass and tipped it slowly up to Gammer's lips. Did she sip or did it just roll down the back of her throat?

As he put down the glass, he caught sight of his mother looking into the mirror. She was running her hands through her coarse, graying hair, smoothing out wrinkles in the shabby lab coat. "So old," she muttered. "Look at me. I really should . . . but with Gammer . . . and the garden . . ."

Jason squinted at her. "What do you mean?" he said, his anger welling up. "Why don't you go back to work?"

"But I can't. There's Gammer."

"Hire someone. Go back to your lab. You're not a housekeeper, a gardener. You're a chemist!"

His mother shook her head hopelessly. "Gammer wouldn't be happy. She didn't like the nurses we had in the city. And it was expensive. Your father complained . . ."

Jason ground his teeth together. What a looney bin he lived in. "You can earn money," he shouted, advancing toward his mother. "You can earn enough to pay for nurses. Go back to work. This place is no good for you."

"Quiet now, Jay," his mother cautioned as she rested one limp hand on his shoulder. "Gammer can't hear her program. . . ."

No use. His mother was in another world. Like Gammer. The anger welled up in him again. Alone. Nowhere to turn. He flung himself from the room and hurtled down the stairs. On his way through the dining room, he grabbed a pot of his mother's beloved geraniums from the table. With furious force he threw the pot at the portrait of his father. It missed. The pot crashed to the floor in a heap of wet dirt and bruised blossoms.

Jason paused, remorseful for a moment. Should he stop and clean it up? No. Why should he? Someone had to have the sense to fight back.

Chapter 3 — Sunday, July 5

"Jason, Sam Slavin is here."

Looking through the screen door to the front porch, Jason could make out the checkered images of his father and Mr. Slavin. He opened the door.

"Hello, sir," he mumbled in his best boys' school manner. A moment ago he had been angry, but he was docile now. Tentatively, he extended one hand to Sam Slavin. He hated himself for submitting to this stupid routine.

Mr. Slavin didn't actually shake the outstretched hand. Instead he took hold of it firmly and looked down into Jason's eyes. Jason tried to withdraw his hand.

"Well, Jason," Mr. Slavin began, "it looks as if you and I have a summer's work cut out for us. I've got to do a major renovation on the art barn. I was wondering how I'd get it done alone. Are you game?"

Jason thought he heard a note of uncertainty in the English teacher's voice. Perhaps Sam Slavin was not all that happy at the idea of having Jason as his apprentice.

"Answer Mr. Slavin," Karl Hurd said impatiently.

"I'm game," Jason repeated mechanically. Numbly he let his eyes survey Sam Slavin. He was a young man —maybe twenty-six at the most. And he looked even younger in Levis than he did in class with his tweed coat and knitted tie. He was tall, but so thin that he seemed almost frail. A wild crop of reddish hair made his head look too heavy for his body. He had a tooth missing—one of the canines. There was no false tooth in its place. Only the gap. That gap had been a source of fascination to the boys at Hawthorne; no one knew just how he had lost the tooth.

Jason was vaguely aware that his father and Mr. Slavin were talking. His father was expounding on a favorite subject. ". . . and I'm sorry she's gone already. Now *she'd* make you one hell of a carpenter's assistant. She's pretty good with her hands. Why, last summer, with just a little help from me, she built new shelves for her closet. But Jason here. I'm beginning to think he ought to learn from someone else. I've never had much success giving him lessons, like swimming or . . ." he gestured at the rifle resting on the porch swing, ". . . shooting. I must not be a very good teacher."

Mr. Slavin's face lit up as he caught sight of the

gun. "Hey, a .22! I used to have one of those." He smiled boyishly at Jason and Karl. "We lived on a farm in Colorado near a town called Akron. There were seven of us children, Jason, and I used to be some shot. The best, except for my sister Betty."

Jason recognized that Mr. Slavin was trying to draw him into the conversation. But he hung back. Annoyed, he turned away and looked out over the vegetable garden.

Mr. Slavin went on. "Yep . . . we had an old Winchester with a bolt like this. You don't see them too much any more."

Karl Hurd was delighted. "So you're a good shot, are you? How about a match?"

Sam Slavin eyed the gun and the line-up of aluminum cans. "Well, I'd like to but I can't. Not today. I promised Roseanne, my wife, that I'd help her out today. She's pregnant, you see, and in her seventh month. And, well, I did say I'd be right back." He bent down and took hold of the gun. "How about another day?"

Jason looked on in disbelief. Wouldn't you know that Karl Hurd had made sure Jason would have another do-it-with-your-hands type, another gun-nut to supervise him?

"Go ahead," Karl urged. "Just take one shot for practice."

Sam Slavin shouldered the gun. "Watch this," he said. "Right through the O in cola." He fired a single shot. The pellet zinged through the O, knocking the can from the fence.

"Hey, you *are* some shot," Karl said with open admiration. "I'll have to brush up to beat you. Sure you won't stay?"

Reluctantly, Mr. Slavin handed the gun over to Jason's father. "No, I can't." He turned and started down the front steps. Nimbus jumped up, growling.

"Dog won't hurt you," Karl said.

"Oh, I'm not worried. I like dogs. On the farm we had a whole pack of them." He stretched out a hand so Nimbus could sniff at it. "I'd have one now, but with the baby coming, I just don't know. And then, we have my sister's little kid with us for the summer. Enough is enough. Well, Jason, I'll be looking for you tomorrow morning about ten. All right?"

Jason nodded grimly. He could already picture the bleak summer. He and his teacher would probably be having their own contests.

"Unless . . ." Sam said hesitantly, "unless you'd like to come back with me now. It was Roseanne's, Mrs. Slavin's, idea really. She suggested I bring you back for lunch today. How about it?"

Jason was taken aback by the offer. He'd never hear the end of it from his father if he refused. "Sure," he forced himself to say. "Why not?"

And that was that. Jason found himself striding along the trail between the Hurd farm and Hawthorne. Every few steps he had to hop to keep up with Mr. Slavin's long-legged, purposeful gait.

As soon as they had left Karl's line of vision, the English teacher's manner became cooler. At least that was Jason's distinct impression.   C797794

After a long period of silence, Mr. Slavin mentioned the Hawthorne swimming pool. "I have to scrape algae from the sides and bottom. Maybe today. It's in bad shape because the filtration system isn't working. I could use some help."

"No," Jason answered. "I don't think I'd be very good at that."

"Oh, that's right. You're the one who doesn't swim."

Jason winced. Was Mr. Slavin sneering?

"Well, forget about the pool," the teacher continued. "I'll do it myself. I was going to do it alone anyway."

After they had walked a little further, Sam Slavin looked over at Jason. "You know, you really shouldn't slouch along like that. Yoga exercises would be good for you. Would you like me to show you some?"

Jason shrugged. "I don't know. I don't think so."

The two lapsed into silence again as they passed the quarry and entered the plum orchard which marked the far boundary of Hawthorne.

The school was actually a colonial-type farm house set in a grove of arching maple trees. The Slavins were living in the small caretaker's cottage attached to the garage. All classes were held in the old house, but there were two newer-looking buildings on the campus.

One was the dormitory; the other was the headmaster's house. The only other buildings at Hawthorne were a corrugated tin tool shed in the orchard and a large, ramshackle barn.

When they reached the front steps of the cottage, Mr. Slavin took Jason by the arm. "Listen," he said in a hushed but urgent voice, "my nephew—the one who's visiting here for the summer. He's just a child, only six, but he's . . . troubled." Mr. Slavin paused. "Well, he's not . . . quite right." He threw up his hands helplessly. "Oh, well, I guess you'll see that for yourself."

Jason pulled back his arm. What did Mr. Slavin's nephew have to do with him?

Turning away, Jason stepped into the kitchen of the cottage. The cabinets stood half-open; dishes were stacked in the sink. A sharp-sweet aroma pinched at Jason's nostrils. There at the kitchen table, a young blond woman stood, kneading a white, spongy mass between her hands. As Jason watched, she rolled it and pounded it down. Clouds of white dust rose up from the table.

"Roseanne," Mr. Slavin said softly, "I've brought the Hurd boy home for lunch, as you suggested. All right?"

Roseanne Slavin looked up in surprise. With her forearm she wiped bits of flour and perspiration from her face. "Why, of course," she said smiling. "Hello, there."

"His name is Jason."

"Hello, Jason. I remember you. Come sit down. I decided to try some bread today. It's warm enough to rise in an hour, I'd guess. But that will delay lunch. Do you mind?"

Jason found himself smiling back at her. He liked the way small, wet blond curls ringed her perspiring face. "Oh, I don't mind waiting," he said.

He had seen her when school was on but never this close. He'd never talked with her before. Now he noticed her voice had an odd lilt to it. Foreign maybe. And she looked different. It wasn't only that she was pregnant. When school was in session she served as the Hawthorne nurse and dressed in a starched white uniform.

He looked down at her sticky hands. "It's all right, Mrs. Slavin. Don't worry about me."

"Oh, please." She laughed. "Please don't call me Mrs. Slavin. Roseanne will do fine." She turned to her husband. "That's all right, isn't it, Sam? 'Mrs. Slavin' is just so formal and stiff. Call me Roseanne."

"All right," the boy agreed. Usually slow at making up his mind, Jason was quick to know he was going to like Roseanne Slavin.

From the time he had entered the kitchen, Jason's attention had been riveted on Roseanne, but now a noise, a tense, dry sob, made him wheel around. There, crouched in the corner behind him, was a small, flaxen-haired boy. He was poised on his haunches—not standing, not sitting. He clutched a piece from a jigsaw puzzle in his stubby-fingered hand. Jason glanced down at the puzzle on the floor and saw that the boy was putting it together upside down. The picture, whatever it might have been, was turned toward the floor, and the boy was struggling to fit the pieces together.

"Oh, do help him, Sam," Roseanne said. "My hands are so gummed up."

"I will. Let me," Jason offered with unaccustomed helpfulness. "What's his name?"

"Buddy," Mr. Slavin answered. "His name is . . . no, Jason, don't touch the puzzle!"

But Jason had already bent down and scooped up a handful of pieces, turning them over so that the picture was visible.

Buddy opened his mouth as if to scream, but no sound came out. He poised there on his haunches, and Jason watched in horror as the child grew rigid. His eyes were blank, staring right through Jason. Like Gammer.

Jason drew back, filled with sudden guilt. Now he'd done it. "I'm sorry. I only wanted to . . . to help," he stammered.

Roseanne reacted quickly. She knelt down by the child and gently turned the pieces back the way they'd been. In an almost inaudible voice, she crooned to Buddy. "See there. There, darling. Right as rain. Just like it was, Buddy. See, Buddy boy. Roseanne has fixed it all for you."

"What's wrong?" Jason cried out, unable to contain himself. "What's wrong with him? What did I do?"

Roseanne and Sam Slavin were both absorbed in an effort to comfort the little boy. "Let me take care of it," Mr. Slavin told his wife. "But you've got to tell me what's best."

"Ask him if he wants to go swimming with you," Roseanne whispered. "He's wet his pants so he'll have to be changed anyway."

Sam bent down and took the child by the hand. "Come on, Buddy. How about a swim before lunch? We'll work on floating again. All right? Come on, Buddy. You love the water. You can splash. All right?" He waited to see if the child would respond.

At last Buddy stood up. His gaze was as vacant as ever, but Mr. Slavin seemed satisfied. "See, he wants to take his swim. You want to come along, Jason?"

Jason shook his head. "No, sir, I'll stay here." He would stay in the kitchen where he could ask Roseanne what was wrong with Buddy.

"Fine," Mr. Slavin said. "Maybe you can help Roseanne with lunch. Come on, Buddy. Let's swim."

Frowning slightly, Jason watched them go. Buddy dragged one hand along the kitchen walls. He walked with a clumsy, rocking gait.

As soon as they had left, Jason turned back toward Roseanne. "What's wrong with him?" he asked. "Mr. Slavin said he was 'troubled.' What does that mean?"

Roseanne gazed down at her bread. By now she had

separated it into three balls. One at a time, she rolled each of the balls into a long strand. She worked slowly and with great patience. "He's sick, poor lamb," she said at last. "He's Sam's sister's child. She and her husband are rodeo people. Trick riders. And she just never had time for Buddy. Maybe she never wanted him." Roseanne started to braid the three rolls of dough into a single loaf. "First they dragged him from motel to motel. Then he was left with his grandmother on the farm in Colorado. Not much of a place for a boy, I'd think. Living with an old lady and no children to play with." Roseanne looked up. "Maybe I shouldn't be talking to you like this. But it's true. That's the way it was."

"But what's *wrong?* Is he retarded or something?"

"No, not at all. Look at the puzzle. Hard enough for a six-year-old but harder still with the picture side down. No, he's bright. Very bright. His problems are mostly emotional, we think. He's getting psychiatric help. He's been in St. Louis at a special school, and he's made wonderful progress. Last year he was able to visit us for weekends sometimes, but I wanted him here for the whole summer." She smiled. "Sam thinks I'm foolish, but I'm sure we can help him if we give him lots of love and attention. If only we could get him to open up—to talk."

"He doesn't talk?" Jason asked incredulously.

"Well, not really. Sometimes he says 'no.' That's about all now. But he can talk. I know he can. Sometimes I hear noises coming from his room. I think maybe he talks to himself." Roseanne opened the oven door. "If we get more heat in this kitchen the bread will rise faster. The school didn't want Buddy here. They weren't sure it would help. But I begged them. After all, I am a nurse. In Chile, with the Peace Corps, I worked with a boy like Buddy."

"Buddy," Jason said. "Is that his real name?"

"No, just a nickname. Benjamin Budke Cassett, they named him, after his father. Betty said he called himself Buddy when he was about two. That was his version of 'Budke.' But that was then. He doesn't call himself anything now."

The braided loaf was rising. Jason learned that it was made with cardamom seeds, according to a recipe that Roseanne's Swedish-born mother had taught her. A Swedish mother, he decided, accounted for Roseanne's slight accent, too.

At last Roseanne seemed satisfied with the size of the loaf. She brushed it lightly with oil and put it into the oven. "Now," she said, "I think I'd better get this place straightened up a bit."

"I'll help," Jason said. Although he felt awkward in a kitchen, he did what he could. At his own house he had never been called upon for kitchen duties. His mother and Gammer had always shared them. Now Myra did most of the cooking, and Jason stayed as far away from the kitchen as possible.

As he dried off the breakfast dishes, he could feel

his own natural tension and reserve slipping away. Roseanne didn't treat him like a twelve-year-old. In fact, she confided in him as though he were an old friend.

As she began to get lunch ready, she joked about Sam's food preferences. "In Chile when we were in the Peace Corps, he read books about Yoga and natural foods. Now he won't eat liverwurst any more. Says it's not pure food—all additives. So he gets organic vegetable salad, and we get liverwurst. He doesn't even approve of my bread because it's made with refined flour. But he overcomes his scruples. He'll eat some of it, just you watch." She made it all sound like a conspiracy between them.

When Mr. Slavin reappeared with Buddy, the child seemed to be calmer. He wasn't smiling. He wouldn't look directly at anyone. But at least his gaze wasn't as blank as it had been. Jason watched as he rocked back across the kitchen, again dragging one hand along the walls.

"Come on," Roseanne called. "It's all ready. Let's sit down."

Mr. Slavin, Roseanne, and Jason all seated themselves. Buddy didn't. He stood watching them out of the corners of his eyes.

"Come on, Buddy," Roseanne coaxed. "Good liverwurst today."

Sam Slavin groaned. "Are you eating that rotten stuff again? No wonder the boy won't sit down!"

Roseanne winked at Jason. "Oh, eat your salad," she said to her husband. "I know what Buddy likes." She reached out and broke off a small piece of Buddy's sandwich. "Here, lamb," she urged, forcing the food between Buddy's partially opened lips. Buddy rocked a little closer to the table. Almost imperceptibly, he chewed the food.

He stood poised there, waiting for Roseanne to push another bite of food between his lips. But she didn't. Instead, she turned away and lifted up her own sandwich. "This is so good," she said to no one in particular. "But Buddy will have to sit down in his place if he wants more."

Buddy didn't move. In fact, it looked as if he hadn't even heard her. Roseanne gave him one last smile. Then she turned to Jason. "Why you haven't begun either. Go on. See how you like my bread. Do you want lemonade or milk?"

Jason chose lemonade. The bread was as good as it had smelled while it was baking. It was faintly warm against his tongue. Mr. Slavin ate it, too. Three slices, Jason noticed. But he was uneasy because of the strange child standing by the table.

"Come on now, Buddy," Mr. Slavin urged, a tinge of impatience showing in his voice.

Buddy didn't look up, but he did speak. "No," he said tonelessly. "No."

Then he began to inch closer. His progress was painfully slow. At last, his shoulder was touching the edge of the table. All of a sudden his body went limp, and he slumped into the empty chair. Using his hands like paws, Buddy grabbed at his sandwich. He pressed the whole thing up against his face. And behind the protective covering of his cupped hands he munched on it.

Chapter 4—Monday, July 6

"Do you sulk like this all the time?" Sam Slavin asked. "Or is this especially for my benefit?"

Jason was so startled by the accusation that he let go of the two-by-four he had been holding. It dropped on Mr. Slavin's foot.

"Damn it. That hurt. Watch what you're doing."

Slowly Jason bent down and retrieved the board. It was his first day as a carpenter's apprentice, and he hadn't made a very auspicious beginning. Only a few minutes before, he'd accidentally released one end of the tape measure, causing it to snap against Mr. Slavin's fingers. And now the board. "I'm sorry, sir," he mumbled with no particular conviction.

Sam Slavin put down his roll of blueprints. "Listen," he said, his voice bristling with irritation, "what are you doing here if you don't want to learn?"

Wonderful little lies—all kinds of likely answers occurred to Jason. But for reasons not entirely clear to himself he said, "My father made me come."

Mr. Slavin frowned. "He made you?"

Jason nodded. His eyes narrowed. "I'm not really the kind of son he expected. I guess I'm not much use here either. I'll go home if you want. . . ."

Jason saw the small surge of pity that registered in Mr. Slavin's eyes. "No, no . . . I won't send you off. We'll work it out together. Your father will be proud of you." He was coaxing Jason as if he were a very small, hurt child.

Jason hated to be pitied. His hands gripped the two-by-four so hard that the knuckles turned white. "I don't care if he's proud of me, *sir*," he said insolently. "I hate all this big man crap—shooting, swimming, barbells, hammering. And you're just like he is. I don't go for that stuff." His voice was getting louder as he lost control of himself. "I'll do what you want. Make shelves, hammer, paint. But don't expect me to like it—or to do it well. I never do anything right. Ask my father. Ask my sister." He lifted the board in his hands and threw it across the barn.

In the doorway was Roseanne, with Buddy standing blankly at her side. Jason froze. He wanted to hide, to burrow into the dirt floor of the barn.

Roseanne broke the silence. "Hello there, Jason," she said, as if nothing had happened. "Buddy wanted to see you two this morning. I thought he could watch you and Sam at work. Do you mind?"

Sam Slavin moved over to the doorway. With absent-minded affection he kissed Roseanne right where the wet blond curls clung to her forehead. "Sure, we'll keep Buddy. Come on, Buddy," he said, stretching out a hand for the child. "Come watch us."

Silently, the child came into the barn, rocking mechanically from side to side as he walked. Roseanne gave Jason a friendly nod. "See you later. You won't mind liver sausage for lunch again, will you? Or would you like a fresh salad?"

Jason relaxed slightly. "Liver sausage is fine," he answered.

With a small wave Roseanne walked off toward the cottage. As soon as she was out of sight, Jason turned back to Mr. Slavin. "I'm sorry, sir," he managed to say in an almost inaudible voice. And he was sorry. But for all the wrong reasons.

Brusquely, Sam Slavin patted him on the shoulder. "Listen, it was my fault, too. I blew off at you. Let's forget it. Start fresh. Okay? I haven't really had a chance to study these plans, and I haven't had a hammer in my hands since we left Chile. I need some time to . . . hey, grab the nails!" Buddy had already dumped two cans of nails onto the floor. He squatted and began to stir through them with one finger.

"You see what we've got on our hands? I spent an hour this morning sorting those nails according to size.

Now they're all mixed up again. Buddy just has to be watched every minute."

Jason bent down to start scooping up the nails. "Oh, forget it," Mr. Slavin said. "The damage is done. If the nails will amuse him for a while, let him have them. Do you like those nails, Buddy? Want a hammer to pound them with?" When Buddy failed to respond, Mr. Slavin turned back to Jason. "Anyway, I'm sorry I got mad. Look, why don't you go outside and find something to do? We'll start after lunch." He paused. "Say, maybe you could take Buddy for a little walk. He likes the woods."

Jason was dubious. He looked over at the child who was rocking like a little tin wind-up toy as he played with the spilled nails. He didn't want to have to look after Buddy, but it might be better than hammering. "What do I do?" he asked. "How do I get him to come with me?"

"That's a good question. I'm never quite sure myself. Well, first—take his hand. Talk softly. He understands when he wants to." Mr. Slavin bent down next to Buddy. "Go with Jason. Take a walk with him. Jason is your friend. He likes you. Then, when you come back, we'll play ball or go for a swim. All right?"

Jason was still hesitant. He didn't know anything about children. Especially children like this. "But what do I do if he gets stiff like he did in your kitchen?"

Sam shrugged. "You saw what we did. Just talk to

him gently until he relaxes again. Are you a chess player?"

"Yeah, I play a little. But what's that got to do with *him?*"

"Well, in chess you try to figure out what your opponent will do before he does it. If you deal with Buddy the same way, you'll be fine."

"Well . . . okay," Jason agreed reluctantly. "But I hope I'm better with him than I am at chess."

"Don't worry. You'll be fine. Just keep away from the quarry."

Still somewhat dubious, Jason reached for Buddy's hand and started to lead him out of the barn. The boy's hand was limp, his eyes registered no emotion, no awareness. In silence, Jason led Buddy across the driveway and down through the plum orchard. When they had passed the tin tool shed at the far end of the orchard, Jason dropped the boy's hand. He knelt down and stared right into Buddy's pale eyes. "Listen, kid," he began, not knowing quite what he was going to say. "You can talk to me. We can be friends. All right? You may not want to talk to your uncle or Roseanne, but you can talk to me." Somehow, Jason expected the child to answer him.

But Buddy didn't answer. He gave no sign that he had even heard. It infuriated Jason to see that blank stare. He suspected that the child was putting on an act. Jason himself acted that way with his father sometimes. "Do you hear me, Buddy? I want you to answer me."

The child remained silent. Jason shouted at him and shook him by the shoulders, but still Buddy was mute, staring past him, rocking slightly from one foot to the other.

At last, strained beyond his limited tolerance, Jason slapped the child across the face. He expected that Buddy would cry out or turn rigid. But the slap produced no visible results. Buddy just stood there by the tin shed, staring right through Jason.

Small red marks appeared in stripes on Buddy's cheek. After a moment, Jason stood up. "Oh, well," he said, "come on. Let's go to the woods."

Jason felt better. For some inexplicable reason he had wanted to hit the child. Now at least he believed what Roseanne had told him. The child was really sick—probably crazy or something.

Soon they reached the small, soggy pond which was Jason's favorite place in the woods. He had been warned to stay away from the quarry, but no one had told him to stay away from the pond. Probably because it was not visible from the path, hidden from sight by a thicket of low-growing trees.

Jason tried to make Buddy sit down, but the child wouldn't sit. As he had done the day before, he placed himself in a squatting position, neither sitting nor standing. Mosquitoes circled him, lighting on his legs and face. He made no attempt to brush them away. Jason slapped at a mosquito on his own leg. "Well, they can just bite you, kid, if you're not smart enough to shake them away."

Jason pulled off his sneakers. He waded into the water and stood very still. Soon he saw something moving in the grass at the edge of the pond. With practiced stealth he lunged out and cupped it between his fingers. It was a tiny frog—a spring peeper. A tadpole last month maybe but now a perfect, fragile little frog. Its sticky feet tickled his hands. He knew that a frog this small would not do well in his terrariums. Either it would refuse to eat mealy worms or some captive skink would eat it.

When Jason glanced over at Buddy, he was surprised to see that the blank stare was momentarily gone. Buddy wouldn't turn his whole head, but he did seem to be watching Jason out of the corners of his eyes. Jason had been determined to ignore the child, but now his resolve softened. He walked over to Buddy and bent down. "I caught a frog," he said.

Buddy rubbed his hands together in an odd circular motion as he squinted to see between Jason's fingers.

"Frog," Jason intoned. "Frog." He spoke as though he were addressing someone who was deaf. Then on an impulse he added, "Do you want to hold him?"

Buddy didn't move. "Oh, well, I'll show you anyway." Jason uncupped his hands and placed the skittish frog on one of Buddy's bare knees. For an instant,

the frog poised there. Buddy stared at it and the frog
returned the stare with its minute, round eyes. Then
with one leap it landed back in the camouflaging grass.

Jason waited for it to jump again. When it did, he
bent down and retrieved it. He turned it over on its
back and stroked softly at its belly. "See," he told
Buddy, "this is how you hypnotize a frog so it will
hold still."

After a few moments, Jason put the frog back on
Buddy's knee. Almost instinctively, he sensed that the
child was pleased. Buddy didn't move, but his eyes followed in an arc when the frog again leaped off into the
grass.

Jason let the frog escape this time. He had a better
idea. He turned over a rotting log. A small salamander
was clinging to its underside. Jason took hold of the
creature. "Salamander," Jason said, enunciating each
syllable carefully. "Salamander. He eats worms and
bugs—just like the frog."

Jason dropped down beside Buddy. He took hold of
one of the boy's hands and turned it so that it was
palm up. Then, deftly, he transferred the salamander to
Buddy's palm. The salamander wouldn't escape quite
as quickly as the frog. He might even play dead for a
moment.

Slowly Buddy took his other hand and raised it. He
extended one finger and tentatively touched the back
of the salamander. Now what? Would the boy squash
it? But Buddy just squatted there, dabbing awkwardly

at the creature's back until it wriggled out of his hand
and back onto the spongy earth by the pond.

Jason scooped up the salamander again. "Come on,"
he said, reaching down for his shoes. "I want to take
this salamander home to the barn. You see, I keep animals like this, just for a few days at a time. I study
them. Come on, Buddy. Get up. We're going to my
barn."

Buddy stood up. Jason took hold of his hand and
led him off through the woods toward the Hurd farm.
As they walked, Jason found that he was talking on
and on. He told Buddy about Templeton and about
the other creatures he had in his makeshift terrariums.
Buddy was silent and unresponsive, but still Jason felt
the urge to keep talking. It wasn't often he felt supe-
rior to anyone.

When they reached the barn, Jason pointed to the
ladder leading up into the loft. "Climb up, Buddy,"
he said. "I'll follow with the salamander. I've got to be
careful not to smash it." He wasn't sure whether the
child would respond to his words, but Buddy did seem
to understand. He reached out and took hold of the
ladder. But he tried to climb with the same rocking
gait he used as he walked, and it didn't work very
well. At last, Jason went up without him, put the
salamander into a terrarium, and hurried back down
to give him a boost. He wasn't quite sure why he was
struggling to get Buddy into the loft. Right then it

just seemed like a good way to use up the rest of the morning.

Once they were up, Buddy crouched in the hay, pale and silent. He showed no interest in Jason's terrariums. There was only one thing in the loft that seemed to catch his attention. Templeton. Once Buddy had seen the small, furry rat, he kept watching it from the corners of his eyes, turning his head slightly so that it was always in his line of sight. At first Jason thought the boy was frightened. Then he decided that it was not fear but fascination.

Jason reached out and unlatched the door of Templeton's cage. The rat bounded out. He scampered around the edges of the loft until he reached the spot where Buddy was squatting.

"Rat," Jason instructed. "This is my pet rat. I've named him Templeton after the rat in a book." As if by way of explanation, Jason dug into the hay and pulled out the old copy of *Charlotte's Web* he kept in the loft. He flipped through until he found a picture of the original Templeton. Buddy didn't even glance at the picture. He was too absorbed in the real rat.

Templeton was always curious. He wiggled his nose and ran between the boy's legs. He tried to untie Buddy's shoelace. Jason laughed. "See, Buddy, he thinks he can steal your lace and hide it away in his cage." Buddy didn't even smile. He just kept watching from the corners of his eyes.

Jason was so absorbed with Buddy and Templeton

that he didn't hear Myra when she came into the barn. "Jay," she called out. "Is that you? I thought you were supposed to be at Hawthorne today working with that Mr. Slavin."

Jason stiffened. Should he answer her or just pretend he wasn't there? "Yeah, I'm here," he admitted grudgingly, "with Slavin's little boy—I mean his nephew. We're coming down." He turned and motioned to Buddy. "Come on, Buddy. We've got to go."

Jason took hold of Templeton, put him back into the cage, and latched it securely. Buddy frowned as he saw the creature shut back into the cage. At least Jason thought he did.

Myra and Nimbus stood below watching Jason descend with the clumsy child. It was a very slow process. "I didn't know you were baby-sitting," she said.

Jason didn't bother to answer. He was too involved in trying to get Buddy down from the loft. When they finally reached the bottom of the ladder, Jason took Buddy's hand and turned him around. Myra gasped as she looked into his pale, staring eyes. "What's wrong with him?" she asked.

"He's sick . . . seeing a psychiatrist. He needs love and help. That's all." Jason reached out and placed a protective arm around Buddy's shoulder. For once Jason knew something Myra didn't. And that pleased him.

Nimbus was suspicious of the strange child. His growl became louder and more menacing, and he began to bark. For a moment Buddy didn't react. Then suddenly he locked his knees and grew rigid again. His mouth opened in horror but no sound came out. He covered his eyes and pressed his thumbs into his ears as if to make the animal disappear.

Jason was overcome with panic at the sight of the child, his eyes and ears covered, his mouth frozen into a silent cry. In fury, he turned on Myra. "Now you've done it. You and that stupid dog. He was fine and now look at him. Look what you've done!"

A moment ago Jason had been strong and in control. Now he was just as enraged and helpless as Buddy.

And Mr. Slavin had to pick that moment to show up. "Where the dickens have you been, Jason? Your mother told me I might find you here. I've been looking all over for you."

Jason stood there, unable to reply. Buddy still had his eyes covered and his mouth open. Only Myra was equal to the occasion. "Hello, Mr. Slavin," she said calmly. "I'm Myra Hurd—Jason's sister. I'm afraid our dog has frightened your little boy. I'm sorry. It was my fault. I think I'd better take the dog away."

Mr. Slavin looked as though he was embarrassed to have lost his temper in front of Myra, but he seemed relieved that she had taken charge of the situation. "Why thank you, Myra," he said. "You're very helpful."

Chalk up another one for Myra, Jason thought.

"I hope you're not going to spend your summer babysitting for Slavin's nephew," Karl Hurd remarked between bites of pancake.

Jason didn't bother to answer. He just poked at the soggy food on his plate.

"Good pancakes, Myra," his father continued. "You're turning into some cook. Isn't she, Ellen?"

Ellen Hurd didn't answer either. Her pancakes lay on the plate untouched. Probably, Jason thought, she hadn't even heard Karl's voice. She'd leave that breakfast, too. She always did. No wonder she was getting thinner and thinner. "After I dress Gammer and fix her up," she said to no one in particular, "I'll put in some new tomato seedlings. It's not too late . . . if we don't get an early frost . . . they'll ripen, I think. . . ."

Jason pushed back his plate. He wouldn't eat the

pancakes either. His were burnt. The only burnt ones on the table. Myra had probably done it deliberately. Well, he'd get even with her.

The phone rang in the kitchen. "I'll get it," Myra volunteered, jumping up.

Jason wanted to leave the table, but he couldn't. Everyone remained seated until Karl Hurd rose, indicating that the meal was over. It was a household rule. Jason could feel his father's eyes boring into him. "No more of that baby-sitting. Do you understand?"

"I understand, sir," Jason said in a barely audible voice.

Silence. Jason clenched and unclenched his fists, as he watched Karl Hurd reach for the fly swatter. With solemn concentration Karl began to pursue the flies buzzing around the table. Swat. Smack. Swat. Jason closed his eyes.

"Not at the table," his mother said softly.

"Oh, come on, Ellen. This is the best time. When else do they all gang up together?"

Before the issue was settled, Myra breezed back into the room. "That was Donny Stotter on the phone," she explained. "You know, his dad owns the Viceroy stable. I saw Donny over there yesterday, and now he's offered me a job—mornings only—exercising horses. For July and August. It's all right, isn't it, Dad? I'll still be able to shop for Mom and help out around here."

"What happened to Warren?" Jason asked, not really expecting an answer.

Karl Hurd smiled at his daughter. "Sure it's all right. It sounds like a great job. How much will they be paying you?"

"I don't know. I'm supposed to go over and talk with Donny's father this morning. Oh, and Donny asked me to the movies tonight. Is that all right?"

"Whatever happened to Warren Price?" Jason asked.

"Maybe Gammer would like some fresh flowers on her window sill. Petunias maybe."

"It wouldn't hurt you to stay home for a change," Karl told Myra.

"Oh, please, Dad. . . ."

"All right. Sure—go on to the movies if you want. But be sure you get things all settled about your working hours and pay while you're at the stable." He reached for his daughter's hand. "I'm proud of you, girl. You can look out for yourself."

Jason didn't look up. That last barb was aimed at him. Score another one for Myra.

Without waiting for permission, Jason stood up and bolted from the room. He'd go to Hawthorne. Right now. It wasn't that he was so anxious to face Sam Slavin again. But he was desperate to get out of the house.

Nimbus growled at him as he leaped off the porch and onto the driveway. Jason hesitated, resisting an impulse to kick out at the dog. After a few steps, he halted again and, on a sudden whim, decided he'd take Templeton with him.

"I—I hope you don't mind," Jason said, as he swung open the screen door of the Slavin cottage. "I brought my pet rat, Templeton. I showed him to Buddy yesterday and Buddy liked him. Well, you know, Mr. Slavin was mad at me for taking him to our farm yesterday, but it wasn't a wasted trip because Buddy was so interested in Templeton. That's why I brought him along today."

Roseanne peered into the cage. "Haven't spent much time around rats, I'm afraid," she said softly. "I used to find dead ones in my water bucket when we were in Chile. And I used to see some rat bites at the clinic. Does he bite?"

"Oh, no," Jason assured her. "Never. He's very friendly. But I won't let him out at all . . . if you're afraid." Jason was beginning to be sorry he'd brought the animal.

Roseanne took the cage and put it on the kitchen table. She made no disparaging comments about Templeton's tail or his bony feet. Instead she studied him through the bars for a moment.

"He's a hooded rat," Jason said. "That's why he's black on his head and neck. He comes from a laboratory. There's no chance of rabies or anything like that."

Roseanne smiled. "Buddy's back in his room working at another puzzle. Why not show me your rat before you take it in to show him? Open the cage, will you? Let's have a closer look."

A series of bumping sounds echoed down the hall. "What's that?" Jason asked quickly.

"Oh, just Buddy, I expect."

"Should I check on him?"

Roseanne shook her head. "Never mind. It sounds like he's throwing books down from the hall shelves again and that's not serious. I can pick them up later."

Jason took Templeton from his cage. Roseanne watched as the rat scrambled over his shoulders and perched on his head. She laughed aloud as he searched through Jason's pocket for a bite of food. Then, after a few minutes, she reached out her hands and took hold of him. Jason was pleased. "Oh," she chuckled, "his nails tickle a bit. Hey, what are you doing, Templeton?"

To Jason's horror, the rat was trying to burrow inside the open neck of her smock. Jason grabbed for him. "All . . . all rats do that," he stammered. "They tunnel, stay away from open spaces. It's instinct—fear, you see. . . ."

"Like Buddy, sort of," Roseanne said. "He does that, too. Follows the walls. Doesn't like to cross in the middle of a room unless someone's holding his hand. Maybe that's why he liked Templeton. Funny he should like the rat when he was so afraid of your dog. Sam said he was terrified."

Jason frowned. He'd almost managed to forget about

Sam Slavin. "Where is he? Is he still mad about yesterday?"

"Oh, of course not," Roseanne said. "He flies off the handle, but then he forgets all about it. He never stays mad. He went in to the lumber yard this morning. Says it may take some time because while he's in town he wants to pick up some library books he needs for work on his doctoral thesis. If you want to you can go home now and come back about one o'clock."

Jason hesitated. He didn't really want to leave. He had nothing special to do.

"What's the matter?" she asked. "Are you disappointed that there's no work to do? You'll be plenty busy before long."

"No, that's not it. Well, maybe . . . I can help you this morning. Help with Buddy. I'd be more careful than I was yesterday."

Roseanne's face lit up. "You know, Jason," she said, "you are a very unusual boy. Not many boys your age would take an interest in Buddy. And, Buddy likes you. I can tell."

Jason flushed with pleasure. But as usual he felt uncertain, apologetic. "I—I tried to make him talk yesterday, but I didn't have any luck."

Roseanne let herself sink down into a kitchen chair. She reached out for Templeton again. "Oh, I wish it were that simple," she said, holding the rat on her knees. "Buddy's got to ease up—remember how to be a child again. At least that's what Mrs. Homans, his therapist, says. I don't know . . . but maybe you can help. Can I put Templeton down on the floor? Will he run off or get into trouble?"

"Oh, no," Jason reassured her. "He'll just clean up the breakfast crumbs and poke around." But he was still thinking about Buddy and Buddy's problems. "I have a grandmother," he said, "a very old one. She can't talk either, and she never gets better. What makes you so sure Buddy can get better?"

"Well, I keep hoping. And Mrs. Homans and the others at the school say so. They think he may be ready to take a big step forward. They say it's encouraging because he talked when he was a baby. And he's friendlier than he used to be. You know, when I read to him he even seems to be paying attention."

Jason and Roseanne sat in comfortable silence around the table. Roseanne didn't demand anything of him. He didn't have to prove himself with her.

Soon Buddy came moving along the walls into the kitchen. He looked at Templeton's empty cage out of the corners of his eyes. Jason lunged out and scooped up the rat, which was behind the trash can chewing on a crust of bread. "Here, Buddy," he said. "I brought Templeton."

Jason expected Buddy to reach for the rat, but he didn't. He just walked out onto the driveway in his slow, rocking gait. He picked up the hose and turned on the water.

Jason felt deflated. "Do you want him doing that?"

"Oh, yes," Roseanne assured him. "He loves water, and it's good for him, Mrs. Homans says."

Jason watched with fascination as Buddy made wet little circles in the dust. "That makes him better—things like that?" he asked incredulously.

Roseanne nodded. "He must be freer. Not afraid. Betty punished him a lot. I think Sam's mother did, too."

"Will you keep him with you?"

"I don't know the answer to that, Jason. All I know is that he's dear to me and I want him to get better."

Jason latched Templeton back in his cage. "Well, let me see what I can do with him. What time do you want us back?"

Roseanne looked up at the clock. "Eleven will do, or twelve. But do watch him all the time. And stay away from the swimming pool and the quarry."

Jason bounded from the cottage. "Come on," he shouted to Buddy, "be freer. Spray me with water. Spray it on me!"

Buddy kept making his wet little circles in the dust. He didn't turn the hose on Jason. He simply dropped it at his feet as though he'd forgotten it existed.

Jason turned off the hose. "Hey, Buddy, catch me. Can you catch me? I'm going to run away." He dodged in and out, hoping to attract Buddy's attention. He knew Roseanne was watching from the kitchen window, and he wanted her to see the efforts he was making.

Then, before Jason could coax him again Buddy lowered his head and butted it fiercely into Jason's stomach. The thrust was so hard and so unexpected that Jason fell backward into the driveway. For a moment, he was angry. He wanted to shake Buddy for making such a fool of him. But he changed his mind when he heard Roseanne's chuckle. "Oh, Jason," she cried, "Buddy only does that to his best friends. That proves how much he likes you!"

Jason was perplexed, but he could feel a smile creeping across his face.

With a wave to Roseanne, he took hold of Buddy's hand and began to lead him toward the orchard, adjusting his long, impatient gait to that of the silent, sober child.

Jason felt good. He wasn't awkward or embarrassed. He wasn't the boy who could do nothing. Roseanne was still watching him. She wanted the child to talk, to get well. And he could do it for her. He knew he could. He knew all about misfits—he lived with a pack of them.

"Come on, Buddy," he said loudly. "We have a whole morning to play!"

Chapter 6 — Tuesday, July 7

"Stay back! Stay back," Jason cried, yanking on Buddy's tense hand.

For some reason, Jason had taken the path that led to the edge of the quarry. There were other trails he could have chosen but, almost perversely, he had followed this one. He hadn't worried that Buddy might fall off the cliffs into the water. He had been confident that he could handle the child. But he simply had not foreseen what would occur when Buddy caught sight of the huge quarry.

The child had changed from limp and passive to tense and excited. He strained and pulled at Jason to take him closer and closer. Suddenly he was a dynamo —wild and uncontrollable, trying to get to the edge. He seemed determined to hurl himself into the glassy water below.

"Stop it," Jason yelled. "Stop that!"

It was so early that no one was swimming yet. Jason clutched at the child with both arms and tried to drag him back away from the quarry. It was ridiculous. How much could Buddy weigh? Fifty pounds maybe? Yet Jason had to muster all his strength to control the flailing arms and legs.

They fell to the ground and rolled in the dust. Buddy scratched and struggled and gnashed his teeth. The sheer force in him was both awful and pathetic. Jason's mind was racing. *In a minute, we'll both be in the water and under it and that will be the end.*

"Please, Buddy, please," he pleaded, copying Roseanne's coaxing tone. "Come on to the woods, Buddy. We'll play in the pond. Remember, Buddy, the salamander and the frog. Oh, Buddy, Buddy, Buddy—listen to me."

Was it his words? Or was it something else? Jason didn't know, but as suddenly as Buddy had grown tense, he went limp. He seemed to have forgotten about the quarry. His stare was vacant and unperturbed. Jason stood up and pulled him to his feet. Then, as quickly as he could manage, he drew Buddy away from the quarry's edge and back into the safety of the woods.

In much the same way as he had the day before, Jason left Buddy squatting at the water's edge while he waded shoeless into the oozing bottom of the pond. Sure, he had promised Roseanne that he'd help

Buddy, but right now he just didn't feel like it. How could he help a child as impossible as this?

He'd find some crayfish today. It would be easier if he'd remembered to bring a slice of bacon or some bologna, but he'd manage. Slowly, he became absorbed in his own thoughts. He stood very still, so still that the small minnows tickled at his toes.

And then he heard it—a hard splash. Without warning, Buddy had thrown himself headfirst into the shallow water of the pond. Stunned, Jason watched. The child, fully clothed and still wearing his shoes, rolled over and over in the water making small inarticulate sounds. They were eerie sounds—almost like some kind of freakish laughter. Jason wanted to jerk at him, pull him from the pond. But he hesitated. He just couldn't make himself reach out for the child.

Instead, on impulse, he threw himself down beside Buddy.

The two of them rolled and thrashed in the muddy water, stirring up all the mulch from the bottom. Then, while Buddy paused to taste a few leaves, Jason ducked his head into the water.

I hope you aren't going to spend your summer baby-sitting for Slavin's nephew. Jason was giddy with the strangeness of the sensation. It pleased him to be doing something that would infuriate his father.

He was startled by something hitting him on the side of his face. A pebble. He felt the sting of another. And another. "Ouch," he cried out. "Cut that out, will you?" Shaking one fist, he pulled himself to his feet. "Listen, I said cut it out."

Buddy didn't pay attention. He just kept pelting Jason with pebbles scooped up from the bottom of the pond. Jason took a pebble in his own hand and lobbed it off Buddy's shoulder. To his surprise, the child lifted up his head and smiled. He wasn't looking at Jason but at a point somewhere in the circle of blue sky above the pond. It was the first smile Jason had ever seen on the little boy's face.

Jason grabbed several more small stones and tossed them at Buddy. But Buddy seemed to have forgotten all about that game. The smile faded from his face.

Jason was disappointed. He reached down and pulled Buddy to his feet. Determined to make the child smile again, he tried to show him how to stand still so that the minnows would suck at his toes, but Buddy kept rocking from one foot to the other.

After a few minutes, Buddy threw himself down in the pond again. Eager to maintain their only means of communication, Jason did the same. Then he had an idea. *Charlotte's Web!* Rolling in the mud reminded him of Wilbur rolling in the mud. Now, for the first time, he understood the piggy pleasure that Wilbur felt. He wanted to rush back to the book to read about Charlotte and Wilbur and Templeton.

"Come on, Buddy," he said. "We're going. I have a book I want to read to you." They'd get the book from the loft, and he'd read it to Buddy. Not for Buddy really—more for himself. But it would be nice to be able to tell Roseanne he'd read to Buddy.

This would be a good time for it. He wouldn't get in trouble for bringing Buddy home this afternoon. His father was at the laboratory in the city. Myra was exercising horses. And his mother? Why she'd never even notice them.

Dripping a wet trail behind them, Jason and Buddy headed back toward the Hurd farm. Buddy stared down at his feet, evidently fascinated with the way his shoes squished at every rocking step.

"Squish-squish," Jason mimicked.

Buddy didn't say anything. He just kept staring at his feet as though he'd never noticed them before.

When they reached the barn, Jason left Buddy behind it while he went to find Nimbus. He didn't want Buddy to be frightened by that dog again today. Nimbus was dozing on the front porch. Jason hooked his fingers around the collar and dragged the drowsy animal off toward the outdoor root cellar. Then, ignoring his growling protest, Jason thrust Nimbus down into the cellar and let the trap door swing shut.

Instead of boosting Buddy up into the loft again, Jason decided they would sit in his mother's car, which was parked in the barn. For some reason Myra hadn't driven it to the stables this morning. Maybe Donny Stotter had come by to pick her up.

Still oozing water, the two muddy boys sat down on

the front seat. Jason was pleased by the mess they were making. Myra would complain, but he didn't care.

Opening the book, he began to read. He read about Fern and how she nursed the little pig with a baby bottle. He read about how she saved Wilbur by arranging for him to live on Uncle Homer's farm. From time to time, he looked up to see if Buddy was listening, but the child's face registered nothing. He was staring at his forefinger, tracing little wet patterns on the muddy seat cover.

Jason read about how Wilbur met the lamb, the goose, the gander, and Templeton. He read the part where Wilbur meets Charlotte, the spider, for the first time. Still, Buddy didn't respond. Jason closed the book. He jumped out of the car and searched until he found a spider. He showed it to Buddy. "Spider," he said. "This is a spider—like Charlotte in the book."

The idea worked. Buddy looked up. He watched as the spider crawled slowly up his arm. He even reached out for it. Jason was excited. He opened the book to a picture of Templeton. "See, Buddy. Here's Templeton the rat, just like my rat Templeton. We left him with Roseanne. Remember?"

But Buddy didn't look at the picture in the book. He was still busy staring at the spider. Obviously, drawings did not interest him as much as living creatures. Jason was annoyed with himself for leaving Templeton at the Slavin cottage. He was stymied. He had no rat, no pig, no lamb, no goose, no gander to show the child. Buddy would understand so much better if he could see them all. He could see Templeton later, but what about the other animals?

The car keys were dangling there. Jason could drive—just down the dirt road to Johansen's. It was only about two miles. They had lambs and pigs and geese. Wasn't it his duty to teach Buddy?

He reached out and switched on the ignition. Buddy stiffened and stopped making circular motions with his finger. "We're going to see animals—like in the book," Jason coaxed. "Sit still now."

This wasn't the first time he had tried out the car. Occasionally when Myra and his father were gone, he had driven up and down the gravel driveway by himself. But he was far from being an expert.

Slowly, sobered by his awareness of the hugeness of the vehicle, Jason backed it out and maneuvered it around. Then, with Buddy sitting stiffly beside him, he edged slowly down the long driveway.

Jason knew that his mother was home, but that didn't worry him. If she saw them leaving, she'd probably just smile vaguely and wave.

It was very easy, really. They didn't meet any other cars. Jason cruised along until he came to the Johansen fence. Then he stopped the car and turned off the ignition.

Buddy squatted outside the fence and stared with fascination at the barnyard animals. Jason talked on and on—explaining about Charlotte's and Templeton's companions. He wasn't sure that Buddy understood his words, but he was glad they had come.

Finally, Jason decided it was time to leave. Roseanne would be expecting them soon. But Buddy wanted to stay. He locked his knees and refused to budge. Jason tried coaxing him. It didn't work. He was afraid to pick the child up, afraid of another wrestling match or of that agonizing silent cry.

Then it came to him. "Roseanne," he whispered, "I'm taking you back to Roseanne. Roseanne wants to see you, Buddy. She'll cry if you don't come. . . ."

That did it. Unassisted, Buddy stood up and took Jason's hand. Jason drove carefully back to the Hurd barn where he parked the car. Then he led Buddy through the woods to Hawthorne.

Sam Slavin was waiting in the yard with Roseanne as Jason and Buddy walked slowly into the school grounds. Jason was stricken. The two boys were wet and muddy. Mr. Slavin had been angry enough yesterday. What would he say today?

Jason prepared himself to be shouted at, but instead of shouting, Sam Slavin began to laugh. "Look, Roseanne. Will you look at that? You and I worry about special schools and educational toys. Look at Buddy. He needs a *boy* to play with."

Although stunned, Jason managed to find his voice. "We went to—to the woods. To a pond. And to a farm where he could see some animals. Oh, and I read him some chapters out of *Charotte's Web.*"

"Look, Roseanne," Mr. Slavin said, dropping to his knees in front of Buddy, "it's good, rich country dirt, my love. I used to play in a pond on our farm with Betty, his mother, when we were children. Jason, you're a genius!"

Chapter 7 — Thursday, July 16

"Tell me, Jason, is Slavin turning you into a car-penter?" It was after dinner and Jason's father was sitting on the front porch, idly swinging a fly swat-ter through the air. "Mosquitoes," he complained. "They're always worse after it rains."

Jason wanted to take a walk. He really hadn't planned to discuss carpentry or mosquitoes with his father.

"Did you hear me, Jason? I don't mean to be nosey. It's just that I'm interested in your work."

"It's coming fine."

"Now wait a minute. Is that all you can tell me?"

Jason shrugged. "Well . . . we've started on the overhead racks. Sort of like a loft. A place to store sup-plies." This was more information than Jason had volunteered in the two weeks he'd been working with

Sam Slavin. But he sensed that he'd be sent to his room for the evening if he didn't offer some description of the job. "And Mr. Slavin is teaching me how to use the power saw."

Not that Jason cared about the power saw. It was just a noisy, boring machine. But his father would feel that using a power saw was a manly occupation, something to build character.

"A power saw! Wonderful. I can't run one of those myself, but, then, I never was very good with my hands. Your mother used to be. Well, I guess she still is—look how her garden flourishes! Maybe you take after her." Karl folded his arms across his chest. "I'm pleased, son. I think this is going to be a good summer for you. Better than you thought, isn't it?"

"Yes, sir."

"Tell me about Slavin. What's he like? What kind of guy is he?"

Jason wasn't sure he could answer that question. At the moment, he could think of only one thing about Sam Slavin that might interest his father. "He likes to play chess. Maybe I'll ask him to play with me sometime."

Jason jumped down off the steps, but his father's voice trailed along after him. "Where are you going?"

"For a walk. In the woods."

"At this time of night? Come on, Jason, use your head. The mosquitoes will eat you alive. Stay here. Maybe I'll play some chess with you."

"Thanks, Dad, but not tonight. I want to go to the woods."

Karl swatted at another insect. "We've got bats up under the eaves again," he said, momentarily changing the subject. "I ought to shoot them out of there."

Jason twisted his hands together behind his back. "But, sir, the last time you did that you made holes in all the guttering."

"Well, I'd be more careful this time," Karl said with a frown. "Now, about that walk in the woods . . ."

"You won't change my mind. I'm still going."

"Well, it's your skin. But be sure you steer clear of the quarry."

Jason had almost vanished from the circle of porchlight when Myra's voice called out after him. "Hey, Jay, do you know how Mom's car got so dirty? I got mud all over my white denims when I went into town before dinner."

Jason stopped and took a deep breath. Simple—he and Buddy and Templeton had taken another ride to Johansen's farm that day. This time Jason had handled the car a little better. Well, one wheel did spin in a ditch on the way home, but they had made it. Too bad he had forgotten to wipe out the car.

"There were rat tracks, too," Myra said.

"All right. All right, I heard you. I was reading in there. So I'll clean it up in the morning."

Myra sighed. "Never mind. I'll do it."

"Now, Jason," his father said, a slight rumble in his

throat, "you know you shouldn't be fooling around in the—"

"Yeah, yeah, yeah, I know. I know." He was sick of this conversation. It was the same old lecture. Without listening to the end of his father's speech, Jason plunged into the woods.

The farther he walked from the farm, the deeper he breathed. At last, completely alone, he felt composed again. He could hear the crickets and tree frogs singing out into the dampness of the summer evening. As he walked, the sky faded darker and darker. Soon, looking up through the branches of the trees, he could make out the first stars.

He was thinking about Roseanne. Tomorrow he was going into St. Louis with her. Mr. Slavin would be doing some research for his thesis so there would be no work on the art barn. Instead, he was to keep Roseanne company while Buddy went for therapy at his school.

Jason liked the damp smell of the evening. He wandered on aimlessly. He considered going over to Hawthorne to peer in the windows and see what the Slavins were doing this evening. But he didn't. The mosquitoes were eating him alive.

He turned back, swinging his arms briskly to fend off the insects. The darker it got, the more vicious they became. They began to fly into his nostrils and ears. Jason hurried along the path.

When he finally reached home, he found that the house was dark except for the yellow porch light. His father always went to bed early when he had to be at the hospital in the morning. Karl Hurd liked to be wide awake to study those cancerous little cells under his microscope. Idly Jason wondered if his father would be more human, more understanding, if he dealt with people all day instead of dead things—blood smears, frozen sections.

Jason climbed up into the loft of the barn. To his surprise, he found that Templeton had a visitor. A wild rat. Nose to nose, the two were getting acquainted. Jason squinted. It was charcoal in color, but that was about all he could be sure of in the dim light.

He knew he should scare the creature away. He didn't want to risk having Templeton pick up rabies from some wild, infected rat. But he didn't move. He held very still and watched. There was something sad about his caged rat straining to find out about the wild, free one. He had often toyed with the idea of just releasing Templeton in the woods, of giving him his freedom. But he knew that was impossible. Templeton was, after all, a tame animal. He would be a victim to the first predator he encountered.

Jason let himself slowly down the ladder and made his way to his own room. He tried to forget about the mosquitoes and remember only the crickets, fireflies, and stars. And he wanted to remember the meeting between Templeton and the wild rat. It was important that he have something interesting to discuss with Roseanne tomorrow. In fact, that had been the whole

purpose of the evening's walk. He would be spending
several hours with her, and he didn't want to bore her.

The details of the walk occupied almost all of Jason's
conversation during the twenty-mile ride into St. Louis.
He even told Roseanne about the raccoon family he'd
seen prowling around the Hurd garbage cans, although
it had been a month since he'd last spotted them.

When Roseanne pulled the battered station wagon
up to the clinic, she invited Jason to come in, too,
and introduced him to Buddy's therapist, Mrs. Homans.
"Jason is only twelve, but he's been giving us a lot
of help with Buddy," Roseanne told the therapist.
"He knows quite a lot about animals and nature—and
he takes Buddy off to the woods. He's even taken him
to see some farm animals. . . ."

At the mention of the farm, Jason grew tense. No
one knew that he and Buddy had made their trips to
Johansen's by car. What if Roseanne turned to him
now and asked how they had gotten there? When she
didn't he relaxed again, drinking in the compliments.
Any praise of Jason was usually qualified by "ifs" and
"buts." *If he would study harder, he might be an
excellent student. If he weren't so awkward with his
hands, he might hit that tin can. If he worked as hard
at swimming as he does at being ornery . . . He could
do it but he doesn't try.*

"And he's been exceptionally patient," Roseanne

continued. Jason winced. Well, patient in front of
Roseanne at least.

". . . He's been reading to Buddy, too. Out of
Charlotte's Web."

Mrs. Homans' smile compressed her face into arcs
of paper-thin wrinkles. She looked Jason right in the
eye. People who looked at you like that wanted something. He felt as if Mrs. Homans were measuring him.
"This boy needs people like Mr. and Mrs. Slavin and
like you, Jason," she said. "With your love and help—
and theirs—he will improve. Maybe you and I could
have a chat some day about ways you could help
Buddy."

Jason smiled nervously. He could see himself reflected in the dark pupils of her eyes. He felt as though
he were transparent. What did she want from him?
Did she want to talk about Buddy—or did she think
he needed therapy?

To Jason's immense relief, Mrs. Homans turned
toward Buddy. "Come on, Buddy," she urged, "let's
go back to the playroom. Mrs. Slavin, you and Jason
can run along now. Buddy and I have some important
things to do this morning, don't we, Buddy? We'll see
you in an hour. Now show me to the playroom,
Buddy."

"No," Buddy whispered. "No." In spite of his words,
Buddy seemed to be very glad to be going off with
Mrs. Homans. His face contorted into some sem-
blance of a grin, and he placed her large hand be-

tween his two small ones—a gesture Jason had never
seen at Hawthorne. In two weeks of watching Buddy,
Jason had learned to focus his attention on the most
minute details of the child's behavior. It wasn't really
that he cared about the boy. Only in a scientific sort
of way. But he did make mental lists of all improve-
ments so he could discuss them with Roseanne.

While Buddy was spending his hour with Mrs. Homans, Jason and Roseanne went to an air-conditioned
drugstore near by. The July heat was too oppressive
for them to walk any distance on the rippling cement
sidewalks. The two of them chuckled together as they
ordered their Cokes. Sam Slavin didn't allow any soft
drinks in his house. He insisted they were poison to
the system.

Jason tried to turn the conversation back onto himself and his interests, but Roseanne was preoccupied
with thoughts of Buddy. "Maybe Templeton can
help," Jason suggested. "Buddy likes him. Maybe he'll
talk for Templeton."

"Well, it's worth a try. Anything is. What about the
reading? Where are you?"

"At the part where Charlotte weaves the web that
says 'SOME PIG.' But I don't know if he hears me.
Sometimes I read the same chapter over again to see if
he notices."

"Does he?"

"I don't know. I *think* he sits quieter the second

time. But I don't know for sure." Jason paused for a moment. "Why do you worry about him so much? Can't his mother help?"

Roseanne sighed. "Betty has given up, I'm afraid. She wants to keep showing her horses. And then, she and Buddy's father are divorced now. She just doesn't feel she has the time." Roseanne took a long sip of her Coke. "My parents traveled, too, when I was little. My father worked for an oil company, and we were everywhere—Sweden, Holland, Australia. But they had time for me. Well, that's not fair. I guess I never had the problems Buddy does. I don't know how to explain Betty. It's hard to understand how a parent could simply lose interest in a child. Simply give up."

Now that was a subject Jason knew all about. But he wouldn't discuss it now. He didn't want sympathy from Roseanne. Only friendship.

The hour went by much too quickly, and then they were back at the clinic again picking up Buddy. Mrs. Homans was saying how improved he seemed in only a few days. Jason was only half-listening as Mrs. Homans walked them out to their car. He wasn't really too interested. Somewhere near by a dog was barking. When a horn sounded, Jason looked up. There was Buddy standing rigidly in the middle of the downtown street. Brakes were screeching and horns sounding. Jason lunged out, lifted Buddy up, and jumped back onto the sidewalk.

He was shaking and angry with himself as he

handed Buddy into Roseanne's arms. It was his fault Buddy had been in the street. The dog. That barking dog. Maybe that was what had sent Buddy running into the traffic. He should have been looking out for the boy.

But Roseanne was elated by what Jason had done. "You saved him," she said, hugging Buddy tightly. "We were so involved in talking we didn't even notice!"

Jason knew he hadn't really been any big hero. The cars had already stopped before he ever went after Buddy.

"You know, Jason, I may be able to make a carpenter out of you yet." Sam Slavin offered one of his rare grins—just wide enough to show the missing tooth.

Jason shrugged. He'd been working with Mr. Slavin for more than three weeks now, and it hadn't been half as bad as he'd imagined. The overhead racks were in place, and they had begun on the new banks of shelving which were going to go all around the walls of the old barn. They had accomplished this much by establishing a kind of nonverbal truce. They were cordial but not particularly friendly.

Jason didn't consider himself much of a carpenter. He'd barely learned the names of the tools. But he did have one specialty—the power saw. Slowly and methodically he'd mastered its use. Now he actually liked its high whine. He felt a distinct sense of accomplishment as he watched it sever a board. And he liked the danger too. One false move and that saw could slice off a couple of fingers. But what he liked best about the saw was its perfection. There was a satisfying precision to the way it did its work. Zip. Zip. Crack.

And then, it was something else to amuse Buddy. Now Buddy often squatted in the barn as they worked. He seemed to want to stay near Jason. Jason was flattered. He had worked hard for Buddy's admiration. The two boys had taken more walks, more car rides together. But nothing had been as consistently successful as the power saw. Most of the time, Jason couldn't be sure whether Buddy was fully aware of what was going on, yet whenever he switched on the saw, Buddy watched him with open-mouthed awe. And the child's eyes spoke for him, alternately squinting and opening wide in reaction to the whining noise of the saw.

Actually, Buddy and the saw had provided the whole basis for an acceptable relationship between Jason and Mr. Slavin. They seldom talked to one another except for "I need the level" or "Hand me some one-and-a-quarter nails." But they both talked to Buddy.

As they worked, Buddy would trace endless circles in the sawdust on the floor. Occasionally he would build intricate towers out of wood scraps, rocking as he worked. Although Jason and Mr. Slavin tried constantly to get the child to talk, they had little success.

The only thing he ever said was "no," and he didn't say that very often.

Sometimes Sam would stop work and bend down to show Buddy how to pound a hammer against a nail. Buddy seemed to like this activity, but he never picked up the hammer without having his uncle's hand to hold his. He would pick up the nails and roll a handful of them between his palms, but he never attempted to nail anything by himself.

This particular Wednesday morning Sam Slavin was determined to make Buddy hammer alone. He took his hand away, leaving the hammer in Buddy's fist. "Now you do it by yourself," he said. "All by yourself. Just try, Buddy. Try."

Buddy uncurled his fingers and let the hammer fall to the floor.

It wasn't funny really, but Jason couldn't help smiling. Mr. Slavin shook his head. "What are you grinning at, Jason? He won't hammer because he's afraid he can't do it alone. And you're not much better. You want to be an expert right away. A person tries and makes mistakes. And little by little he learns. That's how it's done. Not all at once."

Jason turned away. He didn't like being lectured. To his embarrassment the shelf he was trying to fit in was at least an inch and a half too long. He hadn't taken the time to mark the board before he'd severed it.

"Like that shelf, for instance. It doesn't fit because you didn't measure it. Right?"

Right, right, right. Jason pulled out a tape measure and took a pencil from behind his ear. He marked the board. Then, switching on the saw, he trimmed it down to size. Mr. Slavin stood up and helped him swing it back into place. Now it was perfect. "See, Jason, that's it. One step at a time."

Jason worked on in silence. Buddy got up and trudged out into the driveway. He turned on the hose. Jason and Mr. Slavin were both careful to place themselves where they could watch him as they worked. Around and around in awkward circles Buddy spun. "Look at him," Sam Slavin said. "Right out in the middle. Remember how he used to play with his back pressed against the side of the house? Roseanne has done wonders with him."

Jason was already annoyed about the shelf he hadn't marked and about the lecture. Now he resented the fact that Mr. Slavin seemed unaware that he was helping, too.

"And you, Jason. You've been a big help. You seem to have a natural feeling for working with him."

Jason relaxed a little. He turned off the saw and leaned his elbows on the table. "Will you keep Buddy?" he asked abruptly.

Mr. Slavin frowned. "Keep him here with us? No, of course not. At least, I don't think so. We just can't. There's the baby coming in September. How can Roseanne manage Buddy when she'll have an infant to look after? How can we—look out, Jason. He's going for the saw!"

Jason lunged out and grabbed Buddy's hand. In the few minutes that their attention had wavered, Buddy had wandered inside and pressed his fingers against the switch of the power saw. "Where's the hose, Buddy?" Jason asked, purposely avoiding any mention of the machine. "Get it and spray some water. Spray us, okay?"

Buddy seemed to have forgotten why he had come into the barn. He ambled back outside to retrieve his hose. "See," Mr. Slavin said, "that's why we can't keep him. Roseanne's had us to help watch him this summer. But we'll both be in classes come September—and what happens to Buddy then?"

Did Mr. Slavin know that Roseanne often spoke of keeping Buddy, of driving him to school in the city each morning and bringing him home at night? *She* thought it was possible. But then she thought anything was possible—even that Buddy could get all well. Jason was beginning to wonder. There had been so little inprovement.

Mr. Slavin seemed anxious to change the subject. "Oh, by the way, your father has invited me over for that shooting match this afternoon. Says he only works a half day on Wednesdays. He wants us to come about one."

Jason shook his head. "No, thanks. I don't like

guns. And, anyway, I can't work that right-handed bolt. I'll stay here and take Buddy walking."

"Oh, come on. We're only going to shoot at tin cans. Isn't that just what I was saying to you? You don't like to try anything you're not good at. Like swimming or English class or shooting. . . ."

Jason looked away.

"Well? You don't like to hear the truth, do you? You know what I think? I think you're much too tense. You should borrow one of my Yoga books. Try some of those exercises. They'll help you to relax. Would you like that?"

"Sure. I guess so."

"Or chess. Chess is relaxing because you concentrate so hard on the game that you can't worry about anything else." Sam pulled a handkerchief out of his pocket and wiped his forehead. "All this talk about relaxing makes me want to take a break. Okay? Oh, Buddy boy, can we borrow your hose?"

Buddy took the hose and turned it right on them. "Hey, hey," Mr. Slavin sputtered. "Jason, you taught him that trick."

Jason would have expected Mr. Slavin to be angry but for some reason he was amused. Well, it *was* funny. "Sorry," he yelled, as he ducked out of Buddy's range.

After the two of them had persuaded Buddy to let them take drinks from the hose, they sat down on the shady side of the barn. Mr. Slavin sat with his back straight, spreading his knees out so that the soles of his shoes were touching. This was one of his favorite Yoga positions. Jason watched him, hoping that he might try a few minutes of silent meditation. He didn't. Relentlessly, he pursued the subject. "Why are you so damned stubborn? You'd like swimming or hitting a target."

"What about the squirrels and rabbits?"

"What about them?"

"My father likes murdering them."

"Oh, come off it, Jason. You know why he shoots them, don't you?"

"He *says* it's to keep them from ruining my mother's vegetable garden."

"Well, what's wrong with that? We used to shoot rabbits on our farm. For dinner. We just managed to scrape by in those days, after my father died. And anyway, now that foxes and other predators are almost wiped out, we're overrun with rabbits and squirrels. And they've been carrying rabies, too. You know that. You're the nature lover—you must pay attention to this whole balance-of-nature thing."

Jason thought about it for a moment. Mr. Slavin was right about there being too many squirrels and rabbits. He could see that, even if he did hate to admit it. But his father was not concerned with the balance-of-nature, just with the balance-of-power. He wanted to win the game. Prove to himself that he could slay a wild beast—in this case a gray squirrel or a cotton-tail rabbit.

Jason remembered from English classes that Sam Slavin was always ready to speak up about the ecological disasters man was creating. He'd talk on forever once the subject was raised.

"How about the little animals you collect? They eat other living things, don't they? That's all part of the cycle. And your mother's garden? Does she use pesticides? If she does, she's slowly poisoning your rabbits. Is that better than being shot?"

Jason couldn't stay irritated in the face of this boyish enthusiasm. "Hey, how come you don't teach science instead of English if you care so much about all this?"

"Well, I thought of it. My thesis—for my Ph.D.—combines both. I'm writing about Huxley and George Orwell—about the relationship between science and literature in their work."

Jason smiled. So that's why they'd spent so much time reading *Brave New World*. "Listen, don't go shoot with my father today—balance of nature or not."

"I have to. I said I would."

Jason slumped back against the side of the barn, trying to keep the disappointment from showing all over his face. "Well, then you'd better not tell him I'm looking after Buddy. He wouldn't like that. Tell him—tell him—I'm sanding off some shelves."

Sam Slavin arranged his legs into a lotus position. "Are you kidding?"

The skin of Jason's face went taut. "Don't tell him," he repeated.

"You're asking me to lie, Jason. I don't like lying. I never have."

"But this is important. You can't tell him I'm with Buddy."

"You're serious, aren't you? You really *are* afraid of him. Well, all boys of twelve have trouble with their dads. I used to have trouble myself. You know Jim Cellini in your class? He used to tell me about *his* problems."

"Yeah, he told me once. But this is different. My father just doesn't want me playing with Buddy!"

"Come on, Jason, what kind of man would refuse to let you play with my nephew? I don't believe it."

Jason jumped to his feet. He took Buddy's hand and headed for the house. "Well, you'd better believe it," he called back over his shoulder.

Jason was uneasy that afternoon. He was reasonably sure that Sam Slavin would protect him. But he wasn't positive. This would be his last day at Hawthorne if his father found out how much time he'd been spending with Buddy.

Brooding about it, he packed up a picnic lunch for himself and Buddy. Then the two of them set off for the woods.

At the edge of the pond, Jason had managed to build a tree house out of leftover boards. Imitating

Mr. Slavin's efforts, he had even helped Buddy drive in some of the nails. The tree house was a lop-sided platform built into the branches of a low sumac tree. It was, in fact, only a few feet above the ground, but Jason had decided it wouldn't be safe to put Buddy up any higher. To get into the tree house, all Buddy needed was a boost from behind. Once he was up, Jason held onto him so he wouldn't hurl himself down.

Buddy seemed to like the tree house. Smiling slightly, he would rock from one foot to the other, listening to the creak of the loose boards. In some way the sound intrigued him.

"See the blue jay, Buddy," Jason called out as they walked through the woods. Buddy responded by turning his head and lifting up one hand. That was an improvement. Three weeks ago, he would have ignored Jason's words.

Encouraged by this success, Jason tried again. "Look down, Buddy," he said, gesturing toward a squirrel. "What's that?" Buddy pointed at the squirrel. He even contorted his lips as if to form the answer. But no sound came out.

Jason was only mildly discouraged. He had other things on his mind. Today was an important day. Today Jason was planning to read Chapter 21 of *Charlotte's Web*. This was a sad chapter—the one in which Charlotte dies. Maybe it wasn't as sad to him at twelve as it had been at six when Gammer had first read it to him, but it did still make his eyes fill up.

As he boosted Buddy up into the tree house, Jason wondered how the child would react to Charlotte's death. Was Buddy following the story? He liked the farm animals at Johansen's. He was very attached to Templeton. Then, too, he and Jason had spent many hours watching spiders working on their filmy webs. But, still, Jason had his doubts.

Jason opened the book. "Listen to me, Buddy," he said. "This is very important." Then, slowly, he began to read. Soon he was far away. He was at the county fair with Wilbur and Templeton and Charlotte. He knew he was reading aloud and yet his own voice didn't seem to belong to him. It almost seemed as if he were listening to someone else read those beautiful, sad words. And, before he knew it, the end of the chapter was facing him:

> She never moved again. Next day as the ferris wheel was being taken apart and the race horses were being loaded into vans and the entertainers were packing up their belongings and driving away in their trailers, Charlotte died. The Fair Grounds were soon deserted. The sheds and buildings were empty and forlorn. The infield was littered with bottles and trash. Nobody, of the hundreds of people that had visited the Fair, knew that a grey spider had played the most important part of all. No one was with her when she died.

Jason was not prepared for the effect his reading had. When, at last, he looked up through his own tears—he saw tears trickling down Buddy's cheeks. Was Buddy crying because Charlotte had died? This was proof, wasn't it, that he understood?

Jason jumped down out of the tree house and took Buddy in his arms. "You heard me, Buddy! You understood! You're a wonderful, wonderful boy!"

Then, to ease the pain of the loss of Charlotte, he tossed Buddy, fully-clothed, into the pond. It was drier and muddier than it had been three weeks ago, but it was still deep enough to wallow in.

Jason wanted to let Buddy stay at the pond and play, but he also felt he should return to Hawthorne to tell Roseanne about Buddy's tears. "Well, just a few minutes more," he told himself. "I'll let him play just a little longer." Then, looking down, Jason realized that their lunch was beside him untouched. Well, he didn't feel very hungry anyway, and Buddy was too busy to eat.

Buddy pulled some acorns off a low-growing oak tree and threw them into the water. Jason tossed some in, too. "Plop-plop," Jason said echoing the sound they made when they hit the water. "Plop-plop."

Buddy twisted his lips and thrust them forward as though to say it, too, but he didn't. He just threw more acorns.

"Come on, Buddy," Jason urged, too impatient to remain there any longer. "Let's go see Roseanne."

He took Buddy's hand and led him away from the

pond. As they headed back toward Hawthorne, Buddy was unusually attentive. He stopped to listen to a bird singing. He wanted to hear the squish-squish of his wet shoes as he walked. He must have found a dozen spider webs. At each one, he paused, pointing it out with a meaningful nod of his head. Jason wanted to hurry the child along, but he couldn't make himself do it.

When Buddy caught sight of the entrance to a mole's tunnel, he stopped and pointed. For weeks Jason had been showing Buddy this same tunnel as they passed it. Yet until today Buddy had never seemed interested. "This is the mole's front door," Jason explained as Buddy knelt down to take a closer look. "His back door is over there—by the blackberry bushes. I showed it to you. Remember? Remember the picture of the mole I showed you?"

As Jason was talking, he noticed a tiny ball of fur on the ground. He scooped it up and pulled Buddy to his feet. "See this fur? This was probably a mouse that the mole ate." Jason pulled gently at the little wad of hairs. "See? I was right. Here's a little tooth in the middle of the fur. A tooth."

Buddy reached out his hand and took the tiny tooth. He held it very close to his face to examine it.

When they finally reached the orchard, Buddy found something new to interest him. He pulled a few small, hard green plums off the branches of the trees and flung them up at the corrugated tin roof of the shed. Jason pulled off some more plums and did the same. "Ping ping," Jason said, imitating the sound the unripe plums made hitting the roof. "Ping ping." He dropped down to his knees and looked into Buddy's face. "Ping ping. The plums go ping ping. You say it, Buddy. Say it."

Again, Buddy pushed his lips forward as if to mimic Jason. He looked almost as if he were chewing a stiff chunk of bubble gum. He was trying.

These efforts were something new, and now that Jason had seen Buddy's tears they seemed particularly meaningful. "Say it, Buddy. Say it. Ping ping ping." Jason placed his face right up next to Buddy's. He was screaming at the child now. "PING PING PING PING!" But Buddy didn't utter a sound.

Jason stood up. "Oh, come on," he ordered brusquely. It was hopeless. He was wasting his time on a stubborn child. What did a few tears mean anyway? What did it mean if he moved his lips?

Roseanne was in the driveway when they emerged from the orchard. She was painting the bassinet for the new baby. Mr. Slavin was there, too. He must have come back early from the Hurd farm. Now he was sweeping sawdust out of the barn. "Hello, Buddy. Hello, Jason," he called. "Say, Jason—you know your father isn't such a bad guy. Now I didn't tell him you'd been helping with Buddy because I had a better idea. I've invited your family—all of them—over on Sunday. I thought if they got to know us and see Buddy they'd understand why we need your help. All right?"

Jason hardly cared one way or another. "Yeah, sure," he mumbled, going over to get the hose so he could rinse the mud off Buddy and himself.

Roseanne looked up from her work and smiled at Buddy. "Well, Buddy boy, what did you do today? Did you play in the pond again?"

Then, out of nowhere, a strange, hoarse voice said: "PING PING PING PING PING." The words came out slowly, methodically, endlessly: "PING PING PING PING PING PING PING PING."

Jason wheeled around. It was Buddy. Roseanne and Mr. Slavin had already managed to scoop the child up between them. They were both laughing and shouting.

Jason had to shout, too, to be heard. "We threw green plums against the roof of the shed, and they went ping ping. And he cried. Buddy cried real tears, when I read the chapter where Charlotte dies! You hear that ping ping he's saying? That's the way the plums sounded." Jason's words spilled out all jumbled, but he kept repeating himself until he was sure that they understood him. Then Roseanne and Mr. Slavin were hugging him, too.

"This is a special day," Roseanne said. "A special day for our little family!"

Buddy managed to squirm away. He picked up Roseanne's paint brush and threw it hard against the kitchen window. The window splintered. "PING," Buddy shouted triumphantly. "PING PING."

Chapter 9—Sunday, August 2

"Oh, there you are," a soft voice called out. "Buddy and I were about to leave. We rang up at the house, but no one answered."

Jason had offered to help his mother tie up the stringbeans, and the two of them were kneeling in the vegetable garden, almost hidden from view, as Roseanne and Buddy approached. Roseanne was carrying two loaves of cardamom seed bread. Its warm, spicy odor mingled with the humid, muddy smell of the morning dirt. "You must be Mrs. Hurd. I'm Roseanne Slavin. And this is our nephew, Buddy."

Jason smiled up at Roseanne and Buddy. His mother took hold of the fence and pulled herself to her feet. "Yes, I'm Ellen Hurd," she began apologetically, running her hands through her graying hair. "Well, I don't look too presentable this morning . . . You know . . . my old lab coat . . . well, it's good for gardening."

If Roseanne noticed how flustered and incoherent his mother was, she didn't show it. Her manner was as natural and friendly as usual. Buddy stood passively behind Roseanne's smock, rocking slowly back and forth.

"Buddy," Jason whispered, "say 'ping ping.'"

Buddy didn't answer. He didn't even look at Jason. He just kept shifting his weight from one foot to the other.

Ellen Hurd gestured vaguely toward the house. "Would you like a cup of coffee . . . or something? I know I should offer you something . . . maybe milk for the boy. Myra will know if there's any milk. Oh, no—that's right—Myra and the doctor, my husband, that is, have gone off to the filling station. Silly, isn't it, but I always call him 'the doctor'? Why did they go, Jason? Something . . . something about a tire on a bicycle?"

Roseanne shook her head. "Oh, we can't stay," she insisted. "I was just taking Buddy for a walk. We wanted to bring you some of our fresh bread so you can eat it while it's warm. Buddy helped me knead it. Didn't you, Buddy?" She smiled brightly. "Well then, we'll be seeing all of you at our place this afternoon. Remember, you're all invited to swim."

Mrs. Hurd's face was blank for a moment. Then she frowned. "Was that today? Oh, well . . . you see, I have my mother. She's old and not too well. I can't really leave her. You do understand, don't you?"

Roseanne retained her smile. "Of course, I understand. But I'd like to come back and visit with you another time. Can we have that cup of coffee some other day?"

Ellen Hurd's behavior was making Jason nervous. He admired the way Roseanne held up her end of the conversation so effortlessly. His mother hadn't even acknowledged that the cardamom seed bread was there. Roseanne and Buddy had come a long way to offer the bread. The least she could do was say thank you.

Jason jumped up, wiping his hands on his already-muddied jeans, "Here," he volunteered, "I'll take the bread. Oh, it smells good. It sure was nice of Roseanne to make it for us, wasn't it, Ma?"

Mrs. Hurd blinked. "Oh, yes, it certainly was." She stepped back and gestured toward the garden. "I'll send you something . . . some fresh strawberries. Maybe some peas . . . for you and your family. . . ."

If there was any more conversation Jason didn't hear it. He set off in the direction of the house. He had told Roseanne about his father, about Gammer, and about Myra. But he had never described his mother. What could he have said? Talking to her was like talking to someone on the end of a long-distance line.

By the time Jason had deposited the two loaves of warm bread on the kitchen counter and reappeared outside, Roseanne and Buddy had left. Jason avoided the vegetable garden. He didn't feel like tying up any more beans. Giving in to a mood of self-pity, he retreated to the loft. He didn't have many animals right now—just a garter snake in one terrarium and two cricket frogs in another. He hadn't gotten his hands on a box turtle or a snapper all summer.

Jason sprawled on his back. Reaching out, he unlatched Templeton's cage and let the rat climb up onto his bare chest. He tried not to think about Buddy, but Templeton always made him think of Buddy. On Wednesday, Buddy had shouted ping ping over and over again. But since then he had not said a single word. In fact, if anything, the child had seemed worse than before. He wouldn't take Jason's hand and go walking with him. He couldn't be teased into spraying anyone with the hose. It had been a bad week. This afternoon, Myra and his father would finish things off. They'd show Jason up one way or another.

The sharp crack of the rifle startled him. With Templeton on his shoulder, he crawled over to the tiny loft window and peered out. His father was back from the filling station and had already bagged another squirrel. Jason could see it below him in the driveway, one hip obviously shattered. It was struggling to get away. "Get him, Nimbus," Karl Hurd ordered. "Get that squirrel!"

His father had some weird notion that he could teach the schnauzer to retrieve like a real hunting dog. Jason knew it was hopeless. Nimbus couldn't learn to bring the prey lightly back in his mouth. He had another way of doing things.

Jason watched in horror as the dog sprang at the wounded squirrel. With savage determination Nimbus bit into its neck. Then he sank down on his haunches and tore into the squirrel's flesh. Its dark blood stained the graveled driveway.

Jason looked up from the driveway in time to see his father approaching. "Drop it, Nimbus! Do you hear me? Drop that animal." He took off his slim leather shoe and lunged at the dog's rear flank. "Drop it, I say!" The dog obeyed, backing off with a bloody little smile. But he was not cowering. He was still ready to pounce.

"Hey, Jason, are you up in the loft? Come out and bury this thing for me, will you?"

Teeth clamped tightly together, Jason put Templeton back into his cage. Then, slowly, he went down to bury the mauled squirrel. He'd do it all right. He'd bury that squirrel so deep that even Nimbus couldn't dig it up.

His father was still talking. ". . . if you would be patient and take the time to show him, he wouldn't . . ."

Calmly Jason picked up the squirrel and went off to bury it. At the far end of his mother's vegetable garden was a regular animal cemetery for all the rabbits, squirrels, and birds felled by Karl Hurd's .22 rifle.

Jason was determined to avoid an argument with his father today. He didn't want Roseanne and Mr. Slavin to see the two of them in open conflict. When it was time to leave for Hawthorne, he even took his bathing suit.

Despite the short distance, Karl Hurd drove Myra and Jason to Hawthorne. Jason, slouched in the back seat, was reluctant to leave the car. There were too many things that could go wrong today.

Full of apprehension, he went to Buddy's room and changed into his suit. Then, without saying a word to anyone, he carefully lowered himself into the far, deep end of the pool. He stayed there, submerged to his chin, clutching the shiny metallic ladder. He didn't talk to Mr. Slavin or Roseanne. He didn't offer to look after Buddy or help put out the refreshments. He didn't even bother to say hello to Buddy.

From Jason's vantage point, his father and Mr. Slavin appeared to be old friends. They sat together relaxing in the shade while Roseanne and Myra took Buddy into the shallow water.

"Your nephew—is he retarded?" Karl Hurd asked.

"No, we think not. Actually, he seems to be very bright. But, as you know, diagnosis is hard when a child doesn't talk."

"He's mute, is he? Is he aphasic?"

Mr. Slaving ran his hands through his hair. "No, I don't think so, but you might ask Roseanne. She knows more about it than I do because she's at the school twice a week."

"Autistic, then?" Dr. Hurd said. "Did they call him autistic?"

Slowly, Sam nodded. "Yes, maybe that's it."

"Autism is childhood schizophrenia, you know," Karl Hurd continued in his most objective, clinical voice. "Very bleak outlook for these children, I'm afraid. In most cases it requires extensive treatment and often, eventually, total institutionalization. And it's a very expensive proposition, too."

Mr. Slavin nodded again. "His mother—my sister— and her ex-husband are paying all his expenses. Betty says it's a burden, but not as much of a burden as taking care of him."

"But institutionalization is exorbitant."

Jason wondered whether his father was right. For Roseanne's sake, he'd spent the last month trying to change Buddy. And he'd always believed, as she did, that Buddy could be cured. Was it all a little game they'd been playing?

He turned toward Roseanne and Myra. As he had expected, Myra was really turning on the charm. She laughed and swam and chatted amiably with Roseanne. She talked to Buddy. She did all the helpful things that Jason was accustomed to doing. And he hated her for it, seeing in an instant how easy it was to replace him. Roseanne treated Myra as warmly as she always treated him. She didn't even seem to notice that Jason was avoiding her.

Feeling hurt and empty, Jason watched listlessly as his father swam an endless succession of laps, executing smooth racing turns at each end. "Half a mile," Karl Hurd panted as he got out of the pool. "I used to swim half a mile just to warm up when I was competing. But now it really does me in!"

Jason was hoping Roseanne would leave Myra and come over to talk to him, but she didn't. He'd spent a month making a special place for himself with the Slavin family and now, in one afternoon, Myra and his father had managed to wipe it all away. He'd lost again.

Then Jason saw it. There in the deep water was Buddy, not screaming or thrashing, just sinking slowly. Jason tried to cry out, but his voice stuck in his throat. For a moment he thought it was some kind of daydream. Then he realized it was actually happening. How long had Buddy been there?

Hardly aware of what he was doing, Jason pushed off and reached under the water to take hold of Buddy. Opening his eyes under the water, he could see Buddy's own open, staring eyes. He could see Buddy's flaxen hair wafting up through the light streaks in the water. Suddenly Buddy grabbed at his neck, pulling them both down into the darker blue water near the bottom of the pool.

Jason tried to struggle, but Buddy was squeezing the air from his throat. Silently, they continued to sink. The two misfits. Somehow it was almost appropriate. Despite the choking pressure of the water, Jason relaxed. Folding his arms securely around Buddy, he prepared himself to sink with the child.

But then Jason felt pain racing through his head. Karl Hurd was dragging the two boys up from the depths of the pool by the hair. He pulled them out of the water. They had not been under for more than a moment.

Buddy didn't choke or cry out. He just stood there with water dripping off him. From the corners of his eyes, he watched Karl Hurd suspiciously.

Jason's father was ranting at him. "How could you, Jason? Bad enough to have a six-year-old drowning without complicating it by going after him yourself. I saw it all, but it took me a minute to get there. Why? Why did *you* go for him?"

"Thank goodness Dad was strong enough to get them both," Myra said to Roseanne. "What if he'd had to make a choice?"

Jason looked down at Buddy. The child seemed oblivious to the anxious voices. Sometimes Jason wished he could shut out the world as completely as Buddy did.

"You've got to learn to use your head, son. You

must think before you act. Look at this little boy here. What makes you think you're big enough to rescue him?"

Jason was speechless. This was the kind of scene he had wanted to avoid. Feeling as vague and helpless as his mother, he rubbed at his head where it still throbbed.

Roseanne came to his rescue. She knelt down and pressed Buddy's head to her chest. "Oh, Dr. Hurd, it wasn't Jason's fault. He was just trying to help. Buddy must have jumped in the deep water to be near Jason. He worships Jason. Your son is teaching him to talk. Why Wednesday, Jason taught him to say 'ping.' Say it, Buddy, say ping ping."

Buddy nestled his face against Roseanne's rounded stomach. "No, no," he moaned. "No."

Jason shuddered. Roseanne had gone too far. Now his father knew he had been helping with Buddy. He would never be allowed near the Slavins' again.

"Oh, sure, Dr. Hurd, Jason helps out a little when we're working in the barn." Mr. Slavin's voice was casual. "It does help Roseanne if we look after the kid sometimes. Say, why don't you come along and take a look at our handiwork? Change in our room and then Jason and I will show you what we've done."

As soon as Karl Hurd went in to change, Sam Slavin grabbed hold of Jason's arm and pulled him aside. Jason wanted to say some kind of thank you, but Mr. Slavin didn't give him a chance. "So, okay," his teacher said. "You're right. He *is* difficult. But we can work things out, Jason. I'm sure of that. But, Jason, you've got to help, too. You can't just give up."

He turned and started toward the art barn. "Wait," Jason called out.

"What's that?"

Jason hurried after him. "I just wanted to say thanks."

"I don't mind seeing you all day, but since when do we have to put up with you for breakfast, too?" Sam Slavin asked.

Jason shrank from the question. Then, seeing the smile, he realized that Mr. Slavin was teasing. Jason put Templeton's cage down in one corner of the kitchen. "Well . . . I came early because there's supposed to be a storm today," he said. "I thought I'd better get over here before the rain starts."

"We're glad to have you, Jason," Roseanne called out. "Now set yourself a place and have a boiled egg with us. There's an extra one in the pan. And there's a scrap of my Sunday bread, too, if you rummage a bit in the bread box."

Jason found the bread, a bowl, and a spoon. He felt perfectly comfortable joining the Slavins for breakfast.

He'd never done it before but, still, it all seemed so natural.

"Milk milk," chanted Buddy.

Despite all Jason's fears, the boy seemed to be improving. In the last two weeks, he'd started doing a lot of new things. Now he would point to what he wanted. He could ask for his milk. He could imitate the sound of the power saw: EEEEEEEEEEEEEE.

Buddy went over and unlatched Templeton's cage. He would play with the rat for hours at a time. Often when Buddy spoke, he addressed the rat rather than Jason or Roseanne or Mr. Slavin.

Jason jumped up to get the milk. He knew Buddy might not drink it. Sometimes the child said "milk milk" almost as if he were saying "hello hello." But Jason was determined not to pass up any opportunity to encourage the child to talk.

After breakfast, Jason helped Roseanne clear off the dishes. He held Buddy's hands and helped Buddy dry them after they were washed. He could hear the first drops of rain beginning to splatter against the west windows. "Listen, Buddy," he said. "Hear the rain? It goes ping ping against the windows. Why don't you tell Templeton about the rain?"

Buddy was listening. First he stood very still watching the rain from the corners of his eyes. Then he picked up Templeton and took him over to the window. "Ping ping," he told Templeton. "Ping ping ping ping."

Roseanne winked, and Mr. Slavin held up one hand in a V-for-victory sign.

"Good, good, good," Jason told Buddy. "Now say 'rain.' Templeton wants you to say 'rain.'" But Buddy didn't even try. He just took Templeton and sat down under the kitchen table.

Jason wasn't discouraged. One step at a time. That's the way they had to teach Buddy. "Well," he said to Sam, "when do we begin? Do you want me to sand down the new work tables today?"

Sam Slavin slumped into the calico print armchair. "Oh no," he said. "Let's just take the day off. I have some biographical data on Orwell I want to review—some letters. The tables can wait. Just do what you want—you and Buddy."

Jason was delighted to have a whole day to spend with Roseanne and Buddy. He knew that Roseanne wanted to finish up work on the bassinet and get the room all ready for the new baby. It was only a month now until the baby was due. Last week, Jason and Mr. Slavin had painted the baby's room a sunny yellow, and now that the paint smell was gone, Roseanne wanted to arrange things just right.

"Come on," Roseanne said, "let's leave Sam in peace and go out to the barn. You boys can play while I finish lining the bassinet."

So, swinging Buddy between them, Jason and Roseanne hurried through the rain and into the art barn. Jason ran back for Templeton and Roseanne's sewing basket. Then he gave Buddy a hammer. "Would you like to use this?" he asked the child. "Go bang bang with the hammer. Say it, Buddy. Bang bang."

"No," Buddy whispered, pounding the hammer against a loose board. He said "no" but he meant "yes." He no longer turned down any chance to use the hammer—even by himself. That had been another hard-won victory. With singular concentration, he pounded and pounded, blinking his eyes rapidly as he worked. Like the puzzle, the wooden scraps belonged exclusively to Buddy. No one was allowed to touch his heaps of wood.

While Buddy hammered, Jason let Templeton run around in the barn. Sometimes Templeton would scamper over Buddy's wooden contraptions, but that was all right with the child. Templeton was always an exception.

Although Jason continued to talk to Buddy, he couldn't help watching Roseanne as she worked. The light in the barn was dim. The rain drummed on the slanting wooden roof. In one corner a small leak dribbled water into a pile of sawdust. Roseanne sat absorbed in her own thoughts. She was humming to herself as she worked. It was just humid enough so that the damp little curls were forming on her forehead. She was sewing, cutting, pinning a yellow-flowered lining into the baby bed. She was also making a skirt for it.

After a while Roseanne looked up as though suddenly

aware that Jason was watching her. "Would you like to help?" she asked. "You can thread in this yellow ribbon for me, if you like. It's not much of a job for a big strapping boy, but it's better than nothing."

Jason accepted the offer. First he washed his hands in the old basin in the corner. Then he picked up the roll of glossy ribbon. With patience not natural to him, he began to wind the ribbon in and out of the wicker bed.

"Why, hello there," Roseanne called out suddenly. "That baby just gave me such a kick! Jason, put a hand here and feel the baby."

Jason dropped the roll of ribbon in confusion. Nervously he retrieved it again and brushed it off.

"Come on, Jason," Roseanne said, reaching out for his hand. "Right here. There—now you can feel the baby."

Jason shivered as he felt something hard and bony moving under Roseanne's smock. Something was shifting back and forth under his palm. So it was all true, after all. Of course, he'd seen Roseanne get rounder and fuller in the last six weeks, but somehow he'd never let himself believe that there would be any baby but Buddy in the Slavin house. Suddenly, Jason felt frightened. How would there be room for all of them in her life when that new baby arrived?

He drew his hand away. "What about Buddy?" he demanded. "Have you decided? Will you keep him?"

Roseanne glanced over to see if Buddy was listening to them. He wasn't. He was pounding fiercely at the other end of the barn. "I—I just don't know," she said softly. "I'd like to, but Sam thinks it will be too much."

"I'll speak to him," Jason offered. "You've got to keep Buddy. You've got to!"

"I know. I feel that way, too, but Sam and I have to work this out between us. You can't help. . . ."

Jason was determined to speak to Mr. Slavin anyway. Preoccupied with this decision, he drifted through the morning waiting for his chance.

After lunch Roseanne asked if Sam and Jason would move the bassinet into the house. They threw a blanket over it to protect it from the rain and carried it up to the yellow bedroom.

When Roseanne was satisfied that the bassinet was properly placed, she began to show Jason and Buddy and Sam all the little shirts and gowns she'd bought for the new baby. "Do you like this one with the green sprigs on it?" she asked. "Or will that be all wrong if we have a boy?"

Jason stared at the little clothes. That bony, squirming baby in there would fight its way out. Helpless and quivering, it would cry out, demanding all of Roseanne's attention. Where would Buddy fit in? Who would have time for him?

Roseanne tucked the clothes back into the dresser.

"Oh, here. Now you must see the plastic tub . . ." In mid-sentence she glanced down at her watch. "My heavens, it's almost two. I'd better stop this nonsense and drive Buddy in for his therapy."

"No, I'll do it," Sam offered. "I don't want you to have to drive in with all this rain."

Roseanne laughed. "Oh, come now. Don't worry about me. I've got to go anyway because I'm supposed to stop by to see the doctor while Buddy's with Mrs. Homans. Don't worry. I'll drive carefully."

A few minutes later, Roseanne took Buddy's hand and led him out to the old station wagon. Jason stood in the rain and waved good-by. Any other day, he would have been sorry to see them go, but today he was pleased. Their absence would give him a chance to talk to Mr. Slavin.

"Well, now that it's quiet around here, I'm going to try and get some more work done," Sam Slavin declared, sinking back into his easy chair. Balanced across the arms of the chair was a board piled high with books and papers.

Jason couldn't think of any tactful way to broach the subject so he just plopped himself down on the floor and started talking. "You know," he said earnestly, "Roseanne really does want to keep Buddy. She expects to. And he's much better! You can see that for yourself, can't you?"

Mr. Slavin closed his book and pushed the board farther forward. "Yes . . . maybe he is better. Or maybe we just think so because we want to. Yesterday someone in the market took one look and asked me what was wrong with him. So how much better is he really? Oh, yes—and he wet his pants in the store, too."

"But you *know* he's better. Won't he get worse again if you send him back to the school to live? Let him stay here with you and Roseanne."

Mr. Slavin frowned. "Roseanne talks about keeping Buddy, but I'm just not prepared to say what we'll work out for him. Look, Jason, in the last four years I've been a student, a farmer, a carpenter, a teacher. I've become a husband and now I'm about to become a father. My thesis is due in six months. I'm uncertain about so many things. How can I commit myself to Buddy's future?"

"But . . . but you're always so strong, so sure of yourself," Jason said.

"Oh, yes. Sure about how to saw a board or why we should save the peregrine falcon. I'm sure I don't approve of the hormones and antibiotics being fed to the cattle we slaughter for meat. It's the other things that get to me. I'm not sure I belong in teaching. Maybe I just don't have enough patience. And I feel the same doubts about Buddy. I don't seem to have the special touch with him that Roseanne has—that you have."

It made Jason uneasy to have his teacher confiding in him. Sam Slavin sounded almost like another boy rather than a grown man.

Then quite suddenly, he straightened up and pointed a finger at Jason. "But let's not talk about me or about Buddy. Let's talk about you."

Jason tuned out. He didn't need another lecture. But Sam Slavin bent down and took him by the shoulders, forcing Jason to look up at him. "What would you think about boarding at school next year?"

Jason was stunned. "Me? Board here?" He shook his head. "Never. My father would never let me do it. It costs too much."

"Can't he afford the boarding fee?"

"Yeah, sure. I guess he could. But he won't do it. He's tight. He's always talking about money. Mostly about saving it. I don't know if he can afford it or not, but he won't do it."

"Well, I'd like to try anyway—try and convince him that you need a chance to stretch and grow away from your family for a while. You'd like it, wouldn't you?"

"You mean live in the dormitory?"

Mr. Slavin lifted the board off the chair and placed it carefully across his footstool. "Well, not with us. Surely you understand that. We've spent a lot of time together this summer, but if you come to Hawthorne to board, you'd have to live with the other boys."

He moved down onto the floor a short distance away from Jason. Holding his back very straight, he bent his legs into a lotus position. For a few moments he practiced his deep breathing. Then he looked over at Jason again. "Could you do that? Make new friends? Stand on your own?"

"I don't know," Jason said, still absorbed in the newness of the idea. "I might like it if . . . if my dad would ever agree. But what do you care whether I board here or not?"

"Listen, Jason, I like you. I didn't used to, and I guess you knew it. I used to think you were some kind of spoiled, sullen brat. But—I was wrong. You've been a great help to all of us—Roseanne and Buddy and me. And, well, I'd like to help you back. That's all."

Jason smiled self-consciously. Boarding at Hawthorne did sound like a good idea. "Yes," he said, "I think I might like to board. But my father . . ."

"Don't worry. Let me speak to him. I know it's hard, Jason, but you've got to help yourself, too. Show your dad that you've changed and grown this summer. That will be the best way to convince him."

Jason felt a surge of warmth toward Sam Slavin. "You sound as though you know what it's like," he said slowly. "More than I thought."

Mr. Slavin smiled. "I wasn't the eldest in my family either. Remember Betty—Buddy's mother? She made my life pretty miserable sometimes. I was always getting in trouble with my pop for things Betty did."

"Like what?" Jason asked.

"Like my tooth. Did I ever tell you how I lost it?"

"No."

"Well, it was Betty. She shot it out."

"She shot at you?" Jason gasped. "But why?"

"Oh, it's so long ago I hardly remember. I think I told her I hated her. Something like that. It was some kind of argument over the B.B. gun."

"So she shot it—just like that?"

Sam laughed. "Well . . . she said it was an accident. That it had discharged accidentally. And, you know who got punished? Me. Missing tooth and all, pop took his belt to me. He said I was picking on a girl!"

By five when Jason was preparing to go home, the rain and winds were violent. Roseanne and Buddy were safely back, but Roseanne said that she'd heard tornado warnings on the radio. "Jason can't leave in this weather," she insisted.

"Well, I can drive him," Sam offered.

"Oh, no. It's blowing so hard you can hardly see. Just call his house and tell them he'll stay over for the night."

Jason was delighted with the invitation but afraid his father would say no. "Oh, I'll hang around for a while and run for it when the rain lets up," he said. So he waited, hoping that the weather would get worse. And it did. Still, Jason felt he had to make some effort to get himself home. "Well, I think I'll go now," he announced after a while. "I'll leave Templeton with Buddy and run on home."

Buddy, who had been under the kitchen table playing with a box of toothpicks, suddenly jumped up. In his haste, he bumped his head and overturned the table. "No, no," he shouted wildly, ignoring his bumped head. He grabbed onto Jason's tee-shirt. "No," he screamed.

And he was not about to be comforted. He didn't want Jason to leave. That much was very clear. At last, Roseanne took charge. She phoned Ellen Hurd and arranged for Jason to stay.

Roseanne had prepared a sweet-smelling lamb stew. "It's the rosemary that makes it smell like that," she explained. "Say, what about 'Rosemary'? Would that be a good name for a girl? Dr. Roper says the baby will be late—the end of September, at least."

Like a real family, Jason and Buddy and the Slavins sat down to eat their lamb stew. They ate by candlelight because the storm had knocked out all the power lines. Mr. Slavin complained that the stew would have tasted better without the lamb and the rosemary, but Roseanne just laughed and gave him another helping. Jason laughed, too, yet somehow after six weeks of hearing about the hormones and antibiotics being fed to cattle and sheep, he was beginning to lose his taste for meat.

When dinner was over, Jason read to Buddy by candlelight. They had almost finished another E. B. White book—*Stuart Little*. Although Jason tried to read very expressively, Buddy didn't want to sit still and listen. He seemed to be overtired and overexcited by the novelty of having Jason stay for the evening.

"I think," Roseanne said with a sigh, "that you must go to bed now, Buddy."

"No," Buddy cried out, throwing himself to the floor and grasping Jason's leg.

"Yes," Roseanne insisted. "Sam, I just can't lift him tonight. Will you?"

"Sure. Buddy? Buddy, do you hear me? Let go of Jason's leg."

"Never mind, Mr. Slavin," Jason said. "I'll take care of it." He bent down, gently pried Buddy's fingers loose, and picked the child up in his arms. "Come on, Buddy," he said. "I'll put you to bed. How's that? I'll tuck you in. Won't that be nice?"

Buddy relaxed slightly. He didn't say anything, but he did seem to be pleased. Jason carried him to his room. There he undressed the boy, buttoned him into a pair of pajamas, and placed him in bed. "Good night, Buddy," he said. "I'll be here to surprise you when you wake up in the morning."

"No," Buddy said in a flat monotone.

"Oh, yes," Jason answered. "Yes, I will. Now good night."

There was a self-satisfied smile on Jason's face as he strode back into the living room. "Well, Buddy's awfully tired, I think. He ought to go right to sleep."

Roseanne and Sam exchanged a glance. "He may not, Jason," Roseanne cautioned. "Often he doesn't, no matter how tired he is. He's restless even at night. But you mustn't worry. That's just the way he is."

Roseanne was right. For a long time Buddy didn't go to sleep. They could all hear him rocking his bed, and from time to time he would make other kinds of noises.

Jason helped Roseanne clean up the dinner dishes. When they were finished, they could still hear strange sing-song sounds coming from the other end of the hall.

"Should I go check on him?" Jason asked.

"Oh, no," Roseanne said. "Please don't! We're lucky he hasn't been out here yet. Some nights he even wanders upstairs in the pitch dark to find us. Just let him be."

"Well, all right," Jason agreed. "Is there anything else I can do tonight? Is there work in the art barn you want me to do, sir?"

Sam Slavin shook his head. "No, I've got something else in mind. Why don't we tackle that chess game we've been discussing all summer?"

"Well . . ."

"Not 'well.' That's no answer. Let's play."

At first Jason found he had trouble concentrating because of the sounds coming from Buddy's room, but gradually he relaxed and began to enjoy the game. Roseanne sat in a chair knitting and reading. Jason wondered how she could do both things at once. Especially by candlelight.

He felt very contented. Now he knew what the Slavins did in the evening—what a real family did. It was nice. He didn't even mind being checkmated three games in a row.

"Watch out, Mr. Slavin," he warned. "I'm going to practice. Maybe I'll read a book on chess. Then I'll get good enough to beat you."

Sam Slavin laughed. "See here," he said, clearing his throat. "I think the time has come for you to call me Sam. I've had enough of this Mr. Slavin stuff. Besides, 1 don't plan to be beaten at chess by anyone who calls me mister . . . or sir."

So that was that. The last barrier was gone. Now it was Roseanne and Sam. Staring down at the chess board, Jason struggled to find the right words to convey his feelings. Nothing came to mind, so he just started talking. "Well, Sam," he said, "maybe if I do board here, we can schedule chess matches after . . . after school in the afternoons. . . ."

There was a long pause before Sam answered. Then he nodded. "Sure," he said. "Sure." But he didn't sound very convincing. What was it? What was wrong? Jason squinted in the dim light, trying to see his teacher's face more clearly. All he saw was Sam smiling across the table at him.

"What did you say?" Jason asked.

"I said sure. We'll have some more chess games sometime. But now I think we should all turn in. Why don't you try sleeping on the cot in Buddy's room? If he makes too much noise you can come out here and camp on the sofa. All right?"

Jason nodded and started placing the chessmen back in their box. Nothing was wrong. It must have been his imagination. Sam was as open and friendly as he'd been all afternoon.

"Do you need a candle to find your way, Jason?" Roseanne asked.

"Oh, no," he answered quickly. "I'll be just fine."

Sam walked over to the door and flicked at the light switch. "Hey, look. The power is back. It's probably been fixed for hours, and we didn't even know it."

Jason closed his eyes against the sudden glare. He was sorry Sam had touched the light. It was so much nicer with only candlelight.

"Turn it off," Roseanne said. "Don't spoil everything. . . ."

Jason heard the click of the switch. When he opened his eyes, the overhead light was out. "Well, good night," he said. "See you both in the morning."

"No," Buddy protested, clenching and unclenching his fists. His eyes were blinking rapidly as Sam Slavin approached him.

"But, Buddy, why won't you let me do it? Why do you always want Jason? All right, Jason, you push him."

Suppressing a grin, Jason put down his paint brush and bent over to take hold of the little go-cart Sam had just finished making for the child. "Ahrum, ahrummmmm. That's how the racing car goes," Jason said as he shoved the cart. "Ahrum, ahrummmm. Now, Buddy, you make it go!"

"Listen, Jason Hurd, I waste half the morning making a car for the kid, and he won't even let me help. After all, he's *my* nephew. My feelings are very sensitive, you know. After the shoe lace business this morning, this is the last straw."

Jason looked up in time to see the fleeting gap-toothed smile. It was funny the way Buddy had come to depend on Jason. This morning the little boy had walked around with his shoe laces dragging until Jason had volunteered to tie them. Despite repeated offers, he had refused to let either Roseanne or Sam touch them.

Buddy was sitting stiffly on his new toy. Although it had stopped rolling, he made no attempt to move it with his own feet. He just sat there with Templeton nestled against his chest. His lips were moving silently, almost as if he were discussing the situation with the pet rat. He was waiting for Jason to give him another push. With a sigh, Jason obliged. "Now, come on, Buddy. This is the last time. After this you must do it yourself. Ahrum, ahrummmmmm."

Turning back to Sam, Jason said, "Maybe Buddy thinks you've been loafing too much. I spend all morning painting the barn while you fool around with a little toy."

"Yeah, yeah. So I'm lazy. And I didn't work yesterday either. Well, right now, I'd better get up and seal those leaks. It won't do any good to paint in here if the roof is still dripping." He paused with one hand on the ladder. "And, Jason, all kidding aside, you're doing a great job with Buddy. We do appreciate it."

Jason flushed with pleasure. The traces of moodiness which Sam had exhibited the night before had vanished. He had never seemed more friendly than he did this morning.

Glancing over at Buddy, Jason noticed that the little boy was beginning to push the cart with a slight motion of one foot. It was a furtive gesture. Buddy didn't seem to want anyone to see that he could push it without help. Jason motioned for Sam to take a look.

To their amazement, Buddy was even talking. "Rum, rum," he whispered in a flat monotone. "Rum, rum."

"Hear him?" Sam asked.

"Yes, sir. I mean, Sam!"

Jason went back to his painting. They had decided not to paint the loft of the art barn or any of the new shelving—just the walls of the workroom area. Sam felt that some coats of glossy white enamel would make it a better area for displaying finished works.

The painting was boring, so Jason worked as quickly as he could. It took a long time for him to notice that something was wrong. At last it hit him! All the white paint was soaking right into the wood. He'd painted most of the workroom area, but he could barely see where he had been. "Uh . . . Sam, before you go back up that ladder you'd better take a look and tell me what's wrong with my paint."

Sam ran his hands through his unruly hair. "Oh,

no, Jason! You forgot the undercoat! This old wood must be sealed or it just drinks up all the paint. I told you that. I know I did."

Jason groaned. "Oh, no. Why can't I do anything right?"

Sam seemed annoyed but not really angry. "Jason, Jason—one step at a time. In my sleep I hear myself telling you that. There are no easy ways to do anything."

Jason pounded his fist against the wall. For a moment he just looked at the paint which had rubbed off against it. Then he closed his eyes tightly. "But I'm so stupid. I always do things like this. Big help I am to have around!"

"Now stop that," Sam said. "Everyone makes mistakes. It's more work for you this way, but it will turn out. You'll just need an extra coat of paint—maybe two. No use getting worked up over it. And I'll help you." Sam paused thoughtfully. "Look, Jason," he said gently. "I'm not going to be around every time something goes wrong for you. You've got to start remembering these things for yourself."

Jason looked up. Sam would be around. Next year when Jason boarded at Hawthorne, Sam would be there every day. And Sam would give him help if he needed it. He was sure of that.

"Isn't it about time for a lunch break?" Roseanne asked, poking her head into the art barn. "Hey, watch out for Buddy, he's into the paints!"

Buddy was silently pouring paint from one can to another. He seemed to be intrigued with the way the paint slopped over the edges and made wet, white puddles on the floor. Jason rushed over to take charge of the situation, and Sam turned back to Roseanne. "With your usual good timing, my love, you have saved us again. Now Buddy will be cleaned off before he gets into worse trouble, and I can go have lunch just when I was about to get to work." He shrugged. "I haven't done a thing all morning—except that cart for Buddy. And I didn't do anything yesterday either. Oh, yes, and Jason and I have just discovered we have some extra painting to do."

Roseanne smiled. "Well, you're almost finished, aren't you? Except for the paint, what else do you have to do before Labor Day?"

"That's it, I guess. And after all, Jason and I just love to paint."

"About lunch," Roseanne continued. "Are hot dogs all right for you, Jason?"

Jason looked up from where he sat cleaning paint off Buddy's hands. For some reason hot dogs didn't sound very appetizing. He shook his head. "Well . . . if Sam is having a salad . . . maybe I'll have one, too."

"Oh, Jason," Roseanne cried with mock alarm, "are you going vegetarian, too? Now I'll have only Buddy to eat liver sausage and hot dogs with me." Shaking her head, she started back toward the cottage.

"Roseanne," Sam called after her. "What Jason has,

Buddy wants. You'd better fix him a salad, too!" He
turned back to the two boys. "Come on, Jason, he's
clean enough. Let's play ball while Roseanne fixes
lunch."

Jason put the cap back on the tin of turpentine.
"Maybe I should help Roseanne," he said without any
particular conviction. "Oh, well, I'm sure she can make
a few salads without my help. Here's the ball. Take it,
Buddy. Throw it. Say ball. Say it, will you?"

Buddy didn't say anything, but he was happy enough
to throw the ball. As soon as Jason had latched
Templeton back into his cage, he joined Sam and
Buddy out in the driveway. Buddy was running wildly
back and forth in his clumsy, rocking way. He threw a
ball with much spirit but little aim. He seemed to
think that the object of the game was for him to
fling it and for Sam or Jason to retrieve it. All too
often, the ball would get caught in the wisteria vines
growing up against the face of the Slavin cottage.
By now, Jason had become an expert at scaling the
vines to bring it down. Sometimes he suspected that
Buddy threw it up there on purpose, but with Buddy
it was hard to tell.

Jason stayed at Hawthorne as late as he could that
afternoon doing some watering in the gardens around
the headmaster's house. It was close to six by the
time he picked up Templeton's cage and started for
home.

When Jason came out of the woods, he could see

his father sitting on the porch swing drinking a can of Diet Cola and skimming through the pages of a medical journal. "It's about time, son," Karl called out. "I thought maybe you were going to move in over there. First I have trouble getting you to go there—now I have trouble getting you to come home." He paused and took a closer look at Jason. "Hey, does Slavin let you bring that rodent to his place?"

"Sure," Jason answered, glad to have the subject changed. "Buddy plays with him."

"Oh, Buddy plays with him. I see. Say, how is the boy? There's not much hope for him, you know. But, come on now. I'm starved and we've been waiting dinner for you. Stick the cage in the barn and wash up, will you?"

Jason was only mildly piqued at his father's comments. He was convinced that there was hope for Buddy.

He washed up and joined the rest of the family at the dinner table. Myra was very irritable. She slammed his plate down in front of him.

"What's wrong with you?" Jason asked.

"Oh, nothing."

"Come on. It must be something. I haven't even been home. What could I have done?"

Myra sat down across from him. "Warren is picking me up at seven, and I'm going to be late because we had to wait for you."

"Warren?" Jason asked, unfolding his napkin. "I thought it was Donny Stotter now."

"Just eat your dinner, will you, and leave me alone! Isn't it enough that I've cooked it and served it and now I've got to get things cleaned up before Warren comes?"

Jason glanced over at his mother. She was stroking one furry leaf on the geranium in the center of the table. "Oh, that's all right, Myra," she said. "I'll do it, dear. After I finish with Gammer, I'll just run back down and . . ."

"No," Jason insisted, rather surprised at himself. "I'll do it. I can wash a few lousy dishes. So go on, Myra and stop crabbing at me!"

As Jason turned away from Myra, an idea popped into his head. A brainstorm. "Mother?" he said. "Why don't you and Dad go to see a movie tonight? There must be something playing over in Chesterfield. I'll stay here and look after Gammer." It was a perfect plan. He'd get them all out of the house. Then it would be nice and quiet for the rest of the evening. He'd sit and think about how it would be to board at Hawthorne.

Karl Hurd's face brightened. "A movie? I haven't been since we moved to the farm. Would you like that, Ellen?"

"Well . . . I don't know. I suppose I could get Gammer ready early. Could you, Jay, just turn off her TV at nine and give her a little water and turn out the light?"

"Sure, leave it all to me. I'll do the dishes and look after Gammer. Okay?"

"Jason, you're being very thoughtful, and I appreciate it," Karl Hurd said. "I think we'll take you up on your offer. Thank you, son."

Feeling only slightly guilty about his father's misplaced gratitude, Jason began clearing the table. After changing her clothes, Myra came back to the kitchen and watched him silently for a moment.

"I thought you were in such a big hurry," Jason said without turning around.

Myra ignored his remark. "Say, when did you get so good with the dishes?" she asked. "Have you been helping Roseanne Slavin? You know, I could use some help around here—not once a year but on a regular basis."

Jason continued rinsing the soapy dishes. Now, for the first time since he'd come home, his sense of calm was being invaded.

"Why did you act so nice and helpful all of a sudden? What do you want, Jason? You're buttering up Dad for something. What is it?"

Jason was angry now. As though by accident, he flung some water out of a bottle he was rinsing. It splashed at her feet.

"Jason." Myra's voice rose to an ominous pitch. "You did that on purpose!"

Jason smirked. "Oh, Myra, if you want to stay dry and beautiful, you'd better get out of my way."

Myra retreated a few steps. "All right. Take care that you don't get dishpan hands!" she said. "And keep working on Dad."

Jason wanted to hurl more water at her, but instead, he dropped a cup, letting it shatter on the floor. He'd show her he was the same clumsy boy as ever. Why should she know he'd changed this summer? Why should she be the first to know he was planning to move out and live at Hawthorne?

The doorbell rang, breaking off the conversation. It was Warren. After a brief greeting, Myra and Warren went out. Soon after that his father and mother left for town. Ellen had even removed her lab coat for the occasion and had combed her hair. Instead of Jason's old sneakers, she was wearing sandals. Jason was happy to be alone, but at the same time he knew he was doing them both a favor. His mother had been very nervous about leaving Gammer in his hands, yet she had gone. Jason promised he would take good care of her.

Having finished the dishes, he went out onto the porch swing where he sat idly rocking back and forth. The sun set with a red-orange glow behind his mother's vegetable garden. Jason sat there letting the darkness soak in, preparing himself for the big change—for moving away from all the Hurds.

He wanted to wander in the woods, but he had

promised his mother he'd watch Gammer. Although Ellen had insisted that Gammer's bedtime was nine, it was closer to ten by the time Jason managed to drag himself inside and up the back stairs to her room. He took a deep breath and headed for the blaring TV set. He flicked it off. Then, unable to postpone it any longer, he wheeled around to look at Gammer. To his relief, he found that she was already asleep, her wrinkled lids closed tightly over the ever-staring eyes. In fact, she looked almost as if she wasn't breathing.

Jason moved closer. He could hear a faint rattle as she exhaled. She was breathing. For an instant, he remembered the other Gammer—the one who had laughed and read to him. He turned out the light and backed slowly out of the room. "Good-by, Gammer," he whispered.

"See, Buddy. See how smart Templeton is? He won't jump out of the tree house. He'd like to get down, but he won't jump because he thinks it's too far."

Buddy watched the small black and white rat intently as it stood poised at the edge of the platform. A little smile played at the corners of his mouth.

"Come on, Buddy. Templeton wants you to call him. Say 'Come here.' Say 'Come, Templeton.'"

Buddy reached out one hand and ran a finger down the rat's pink, bony tail. "Rum, rum, rum, rum," he said in a faraway sing-song voice.

Jason was pleased. He hadn't gotten the response he sought, but at least Buddy had answered. Buddy was noticeably better than he had been two months ago. Gone was the blank stare, gone were the rigid fits. Well, almost gone.

Still, Jason was worried. As he chattered for Buddy, he mulled over the same old problems. It was almost Labor Day—and as far as Jason knew, no decision had been made about keeping Buddy. To make it all worse, Karl Hurd was still *considering* whether he'd let Jason board at Hawthorne. It had been almost a week now since he and Sam had discussed the matter, and the longer Jason waited for his father's decision, the more convinced he became that the answer would be no.

Buddy was better, all right. But he wasn't normal by any definition. He still threw things, still screamed "no" when he was crossed, still had to be watched so that he stayed away from the pool and from the quarry and from the power saw. Jason didn't like to admit how difficult Buddy was. Only someone who loved him could overlook all his shortcomings. And Jason had finally come to see how important Buddy was to him—just because of Buddy—not because of Roseanne or Sam.

Buddy was the first person who had ever needed Jason. He followed Jason everywhere. He wore his tee-shirt untucked like Jason. He kept a pencil behind his ear like Jason. Roseanne said he always sulked at night when Jason and Templeton headed for home.

Jason was getting more and more concerned about what would happen if the Slavins just sent Buddy back to his school in the city. He began to feel it was absolutely necessary that Buddy make some new and dramatic improvement to convince them that he mustn't be sent away.

Jason had been putting it off, but today he and Buddy were going to have a serious talk. He had chosen the tree house as the ideal location. And he'd made sure that Templeton was along to help.

For a while longer, Jason delayed. He tried to show Buddy how to tie his own shoes. He almost had it. "Come on, Buddy boy. Do it for me. For Jason. Do it for Templeton. Show him."

At last, Jason could wait no longer. He sat cross-legged, facing Buddy. "Now, Buddy," he began softly. "This is very important, and you must listen. Look at Templeton up on his hind legs. He's listening, and he wants you to listen."

Buddy looked at Templeton with his odd little smile, but he wouldn't look at Jason.

"Listen like when I read to you, Buddy. You've just got to talk. Really talk. Do you understand? Not just a word here and there and then forgetting what you've said. Not just whispering to Templeton or talking in your room at night when you're alone." Jason paused. "You see, Buddy, the summer's almost gone. If you're not better, then . . . then . . ." He didn't want to say it, but he had to. "Buddy, Roseanne and your uncle—they won't keep you here if you don't talk. They'll send you away, back to your old school to live. You like Mrs. Homans, but do you want to live

there at her school again? Is that what you want? Do
you want to go away and never come back?"

Buddy's face was somber but unemotional. One
hand stroked Templeton softly, but his body was still
and unresponsive.

"Do you hear me, Buddy?" There was more urgency
creeping into Jason's voice now. "Remember *Stuart
Little?* Stuart was a mouse, wasn't he, born into a
human family? He was different . . . and, well, you're
different, too, Buddy. But Stuart talked and the family
in the book kept him, didn't they? Don't you want
Roseanne and Sam to keep you? Come on, Buddy
boy. I know you can talk. Say my name: Jason. Say
yours: Buddy. See that bird up in the tree? Say bird.
Say tree. Say something. Anything! You've got to do it,
Buddy!"

Yelling at Buddy had never helped, and now Jason
found that he was yelling again. He didn't want to.
He just didn't know what else to do. Buddy wasn't
responding. Jason picked up Templeton. "Templeton
wants you to say Buddy. Tell Templeton your name.
If you can't, I'll take Templeton away, and you'll
never see him again. You wouldn't like that, would
you?"

Buddy was silent. He just sat there rotating his
thumbs in circles around each other. Jason was running
out of ideas. Then something stirred in his head. It
was crazy, he knew that, but it might work and anything that might work was worth a try.

"Come on, Buddy," Jason said, lowering his voice again. "I want you to meet somebody. I have someone at my house who wants to meet you."

Ordinarily Jason would not have risked taking Buddy to the Hurd house on a Wednesday afternoon. Wednesday was a half day at the office for Karl Hurd. But this particular Wednesday Jason happened to know that his father had plans. First a meeting with a real estate agent in Viceroy and then he'd promised Myra he'd meet her at the quarry for a swim.

So, holding Templeton's cage in one hand and Buddy's fist in the other, Jason walked through the woods toward the Hurd farm. He knew they wouldn't see his mother at this time of day. She'd be in her room taking a nap. As they headed up the back stairs, Jason could hear the TV set.

Silently the two boys walked down the long hall and into Gammer's room. As usual, Gammer was strapped into the rocking chair. Her gaze was blank. The pale eyes stared at the flickering television set. Jason placed Buddy between Gammer and the TV. He turned Buddy's head so that the child was forced to look right into the old woman's vacant eyes.

Jason's voice rose high enough to be heard over the blare of the television. "See, Buddy. That's my grandmother—we call her Gammer. She's old . . . and she's like you, Buddy. You want to know how an old woman can be like you? Look at her eyes. Your eyes look that way sometimes. She never says anything.

Not one word. All day she sits strapped there until it's time to go to bed." Jason knelt down so that his mouth was very close to Buddy's ears. "You've got to talk, Buddy. Do you understand? Do you want to be like that? Forever—until you die? Do you? Do you?"

Buddy's knees locked, and he started to rock from side to side. Then, in terror, he covered his eyes and pressed his thumbs into his ears. "No, no, no," he screamed. "NO, NO, NO, NO, NO!"

Over and over again, the child repeated that one word. "NO, NO, NO, NO, NO . . ." His voice was hoarse and monotonous. "NO, NO, NO, NO, NO . . ."

Jason was suddenly aware of the sound of crepe soles. Then his father's voice bellowed out, "What the hell is going on in here?"

Karl Hurd reached out and flipped off the television set. "What is that child doing here? And what are you doing here, Jason? You're supposed to be hammering or something." Karl looked angrily from Buddy to Gammer. "So that's it. What is this, amateur psychiatrist day? Amateur shock therapy? Jason, this boy is a schizophrenic. Do you think you can cure him just by exposing him to Gammer?"

Buddy continued to stand there, shouting his one word over and over without pause. "NO, NO, NO, NO . . ."

"You can't cure him, Jason," Karl Hurd said, slowly regaining his composure. "Maybe no one can but certainly not you. Seeing Gammer here will probably set him back six months. You may think you've had me fooled. You think I don't know what you've been doing this summer. Sure, I saw those shelves and things you built, but that's not a summer's work. You think I don't know you've been working with the boy most of the time? Well, let me tell you, it's all hopeless. Now, take him home. And get that god-damned rat out of here. You know he's not supposed to be in the house."

Jason was watching Buddy. He wanted to see if Buddy heard any of what Karl Hurd was saying. Probably not. He was too busy screaming—yet as soon as the rat was mentioned, he stopped screaming and pulled his hands away from his face. Out of the corners of his eyes, he stared at Templeton. Then he stared at Gammer. Then at Karl. Then back at Gammer.

"Did you hear me, Jason? Get that rat out of my sight before I wring his neck. And, look at the child. He's wetting himself, and it's getting all over Gammer's rug. Now you'll have something to clean up before you take him home."

"I'll clean it up, Jay," a voice said softly from the hallway. It was Myra, her hair still wet from swimming in the quarry. She'd been there the whole time, listening. "You go on and take Buddy home, and I'll clean up the rug."

Jason held his breath for a moment, but it didn't work. He still exploded. "Shut up, Myra. If you're going to do it, do it. But shut up about it. Come on, Buddy, you and me and Templeton are getting out of here!"

Jason was confused. His experiment had been a failure. Not only had it terrified Buddy, but he'd been caught. And it hurt to admit that his father was right. He *had* been playing amateur psychiatrist. Buddy was a mess. His face was blank, his limbs rigid, his pants wet.

With Templeton's cage wedged under one arm, Jason led Buddy from the room and down the stairs. Nimbus jumped up and growled at them on the way out. Jason slammed the screen door half hoping it would smack the dog on the tender end of his nose. For once Buddy didn't even seem to notice the dog. He was back in his own safe, silent world.

First Jason put Templeton's cage up in the loft. Then, deeply discouraged and depressed, he led Buddy home. The child's hand lay limply in his. Clumsily Buddy rocked along, seemingly unaware of the dark stain marking the front of his faded jeans.

Sam Slavin was waiting for them. He was standing impatiently in the yard, his mouth set firmly. His eyes were snapping mad.

"Come here, Buddy," he called, his anger barely contained. "Go inside to Roseanne. Roseanne wants you."

Buddy dropped Jason's hand and went slowly rocking over to the cottage door. Roseanne opened it and led him in. She didn't look up at Jason at all.

As soon as the door was closed, Sam started shouting. "Your father called me," he said, shaking with anger. "I hear you've been trying to cure Buddy all by yourself! What do you mean by taking him there and upsetting him like that? Did you see him? He looked awful. What were you thinking of?"

Jason felt empty, passive. Not angry. Listening to Sam Slavin tell him off was no different than listening to his own father. But he expected nothing from his father. He had thought Sam was his friend.

He waited until his teacher had finished. Then, without any spirit or will, he answered, "But I only wanted Buddy to talk. I wanted him well so you wouldn't send him away."

"Oh, God. Not that again. Listen here, Jason, what we do or don't decide about Buddy is none of your business. If we keep him, it's because we want to, not because he talks or doesn't talk. Or because of what you think. It's between Roseanne and me. Just the two of us. No matter what you think, you're not part of this family." Sam shook his head. "I knew we were making a mistake with you. I could see it all along, but I didn't have the heart to put a stop to it. It was nice this summer, but there was too much—too much interfering. Now let us worry about Buddy. Understand?"

Jason understood. His shoulders sagging, he turned away.

"And, Jason, one more thing. Maybe you shouldn't come back before school starts. Buddy was so disturbed. It may not be good for him to have you back." Then, for a moment, Sam's face softened. "However, this won't change my feelings about you boarding at Hawthorne. In fact, more than ever, I see you need it. You need something. That's for sure!"

That was it. Jason headed slowly back along the trail toward his own farm. Now there was nothing. He had ruined everything.

Chapter 14—Saturday, August 29

"Cut it out, Templeton," Jason said irritably. "Can't you see I don't feel like playing this morning?"

Jason was stretched on his stomach in the loft. He was annoyed that Templeton had chosen this particular morning to be interested in his bare toes. Jason wanted to sulk, but the rat kept tickling his feet.

Abruptly, he picked Templeton up by the scruff of his neck and latched him back in the wire cage. Near the cage he noticed a stack of books borrowed from Sam Slavin. Angry with himself and with Sam all over again, he took a mound of hay and buried the books so that he wouldn't have to look at them. He turned away from Templeton, too. Templeton reminded him of Buddy.

He glanced over at his empty terrariums. He hadn't

had time to collect any wildlife lately. Buddy had been more important than any newt or turtle. Thursday, Friday, and most of Saturday. He could have spent these three days in the woods gathering up specimens for studying over the Labor Day weekend. But he hadn't gone to the woods. Instead, he'd spent the time in the loft, in his bedroom, by himself. He'd been hoping that Sam Slavin would call or come and apologize—invite him back to Hawthorne. Maybe Buddy needed Jason. Maybe Buddy was crying for him, unable to understand why both Jason and Templeton had disappeared. But there was no call from the Slavins.

He peered mournfully out of the loft window. His father was lifting barbells on the front porch. He and Myra had already been swimming in the quarry. Or riding or bicycling or something.

"There he is next to the tomatoes," Karl Hurd's voice boomed out. "Get him, Myra."

Jason's attention focused on Myra. Now here was something new. Myra, to his knowledge, had never yet shot at an animal, only at cola cans on the fence. He wondered if she would do it. Jason stiffened. Yes, of course, she'd do it. She'd do anything to please her father.

Silently Jason urged the rabbit to run, but it poked along, unaware that Myra was taking hold of the gun, shouldering it, lining up her aim. Stupid rabbit. It was giving her all the time she needed.

Not bothering to use the ladder, Jason hurled himself down from the loft. He ran toward the garden screaming at Myra, but her shot had already gone off. Just one shot and the rabbit lay there, quivering slightly. Jason lunged down and scooped up the throbbing body, holding it away from Nimbus who was already advancing rapidly from the front porch. "Hey, Myra," he taunted, hardly hearing the sound of his own voice. His head was pounding, and he could feel a pulse throbbing at the base of his neck. "Shoot me. Why don't you shoot me? Shoot me through the head, too."

Karl Hurd stood on the front porch, a barbell poised above his head. For once he seemed to be at a loss for words. He didn't yell at Jason. He just stared. Then slowly, and with proper form, he lowered the barbell to the floor. Taking a pocket handkerchief from his pants, he wiped his perspiring forehead. "Put the gun away, Myra," he said in a low voice. "And, Jason, you go bury the rabbit, will you? Right now."

Jason lowered his arms and cradled the dead rabbit to his chest. The pellet had entered cleanly. There was only a small hole. Blood oozed from the head as he shifted his grip on the animal. Slowly Jason retreated. He didn't turn his back on his father. He just kept backing up and backing up until he was behind the barn and out of sight. Then he took the dead rabbit and carried it gently up to the loft.

Brooding and hating, Jason stayed in the loft for the rest of the day.

Much later, Myra came out to call him for dinner. Jason didn't answer.

"There won't be any dinner if you don't come now," she said. "You didn't have lunch so you must be hungry."

Jason didn't move.

"Listen to me, Jason. I didn't want to shoot that rabbit, but Dad was so insistent. You know how he gets. Listen, stop feeling so sorry for yourself. What about me? Dad's hard to please and Mom—she's no help anymore. I seem to get stuck with everything. Why do you think I spend so much time away from here? Do you know what I'm talking about, Jason?"

Jason didn't budge. She hadn't really come out to call him to dinner. She had come to complain.

"I've made spaghetti," Myra called. "I thought you liked spaghetti. What's wrong with you? Can't you even answer?"

"No," Jason muttered.

"But, Jay," she began. Then she seemed to change her mind. "Oh, forget it." Jason could hear rapid footsteps carrying her toward the house. The screen door slammed as she went back in.

Jason could picture them at dinner. Karl would be discussing the thrill of seeing Myra shoot her first rabbit. *What a terrific shot you are, Myra. And with a moving target, too. You really surprised me.* Some moving target. A slow, dumb snuffling rabbit.

And his mother? Would she miss him at dinner? Would she even know he wasn't there? A dry, tight laugh exploded in his throat as he imagined his mother's voice. *Well, has Jason come? He didn't? He fell into the quarry? Well, if that's what he wanted to do . . . but he could have done it on a day Gammer was feeling . . . oh, and I did want him to pick some peas before. . . .*

He glanced over at the rabbit. Rigor mortis had set in. It was stiff and cold. He knew he should bury it, back in the usual place behind the vegetable garden. But he hesitated. And, suddenly he knew what it was he wanted to do. Taking hold of the dead rabbit, he descended from the loft. He went around to the back entrance of the farm house. Silently, on bare feet, he went through the kitchen. He could hear the drone of his father's voice and the lilt of Myra's. Under his feet he felt cool tile, bare boards, worn carpet. He went past Gammer's room, closing his eyes so he wouldn't see her and made his way to Myra's room.

Kneeling down, he pulled back the bedspread and the blue blanket just enough so that he could nestle the dead rabbit under her pillow. Then, with slow, meticulous care, he remade the bed. He smoothed every wrinkle out of the chenille spread. He replaced Myra's purple stuffed octopus just as it had been, with its legs smugly crossed.

As soon as he had left the house, a devastating thought struck him. He'd made a mistake. That rabbit belonged in his father's bed, not in Myra's! He'd bungled another job. He had stopped, ready to go back again, when he heard the dining chairs scraping against the bare floor. He waited one more instant. Then he started to run toward the woods.

Wandering aimlessly, he found his way to the tree house. When he looked at it objectively, he saw that it was a flimsy contraption. Who ever heard of a tree house two feet off the ground? It was another bungled job. He didn't want to sit in the tree house, but there was nowhere else to go. He preferred not to be in the house or in the loft when Myra discovered what was under her pillow.

He sat down on the wobbly platform. "Damn," he muttered, looking at a long splinter he'd gouged under the nail of his big toe. He didn't bother to pull out the splinter. He just sat there idly, letting the darkness fall. It was beginning to darken earlier now that the summer was almost over. Oddly enough there were no mosquitoes around. A stiff, cool wind was blowing from the north. Jason shivered in his tee-shirt and jeans. He felt strangely light-headed. Was it because he hadn't eaten?

After a long while, he grew restless. He thought maybe he'd sneak over to Hawthorne and peer in the windows of the cottage. Maybe he would see the Slavins and Buddy. Maybe he could hear what Roseanne and Sam were talking about.

He made his way through the dark woods toward Hawthorne, choosing the path along the edge of the quarry. He walked close to the edge, acutely aware of the black canyon gaping below. A skunk with her three young crossed the path ahead of him. The white stripes glinted despite the dimness. Another night, he would have studied the skunks in order to tell Roseanne about them, but tonight he ignored them.

He hurried on past the quarry and into the plum orchard. He was surprised to see that the downstairs lights were already turned off. Was it that late already? Buddy's room was dark, its shades drawn. Jason peered over toward the headmaster's house. It, too, was dark. No one would be there until after Labor Day.

The only light that showed came from the window of Sam and Roseanne's room. Jason stared at the rectangle of light reflected obliquely on the driveway. Well, the shade wasn't drawn, was it? He looked at the wisteria vines clinging to the front of the white cottage. He could just climb up those vines and have a quick look. The window was open. He could peer in silently and hear what they were saying. It was so windy that no one would notice the creaking of the vines. And, even if he got caught, what difference did it make? But, still, he waited.

Then, at last, for lack of a better idea, Jason climbed slowly up the wisteria. He knew it would hold him. It was anchored to the house with metal hooks. And he had climbed it often enough to retrieve Buddy's ball.

Hand over hand he inched his way up, feeling for each secure grip. Finally his eyes were on a level with the window. He blinked, blinded at first by the brightness. Sam was sitting on the floor in some Yoga position, a book propped open in front of him. Roseanne was in a robe. She was sitting up in bed brushing her hair with short, expert jabs. From time to time she would stop brushing and press her hands against her large, rounded stomach.

Jason waited there, the rough vines digging into his fingers. He waited for them to talk about him, about Buddy. Their voices were low, but he could make them out. Roseanne talked only about the new baby. It was kicking. "Why especially at night when I want to sleep?" She laughed. "Oh, Sam, are you listening to me? We really must pick out a name."

"Yeah, I'm listening," he answered, turning another page in his book. "There's a stiff wind blowing. The weather will change. Do you want me to close the window in case we get some rain?"

"No, leave it," Roseanne said, flipping her brush aside and taking up a pair of toenail clippers. "What's that book? *Catcher in the Rye?* Have you decided?

Is that what you're going to start with for the ninth grade?"

"Oh, I don't know. Honestly, I don't know. Some nights I don't seem to know about anything."

"Listen, Sam, should we chuck it all? Go find a farm to live on where you can do research and write books?"

Sam made a face. "Roseanne, you have great ideas, but you are *so* impractical. What would we do for money if I wasn't working? How would we get by?"

"Why . . . I'd bake bread," Roseanne teased, "and take it to market every week. . . ."

Jason waited. He waited for an eternity. But their conversation drifted on aimlessly. No mention of him. No mention of Buddy. They didn't care about anyone except themselves and that new baby. He could see that.

At last, stiff and despondent, he picked his way back down the wisteria and dropped to the ground. Then, with so little will that the wind could have been blowing him, he drifted home. He wandered in the front door, blinking again at the sharp light here. He didn't slam the door. He didn't say goodnight to anyone. He made his way upstairs past Gammer's room, past Myra's room, and flung himself listlessly into his own bed.

Chapter 15—Sunday, August 30

It was morning already. Last night Jason had waited sleeplessly for Myra to scream when she found the dead rabbit. But he hadn't heard any screaming. Through the connecting wall he could hear her moving around. He had listened as she opened and closed drawers. He was jarred by the sound of the lid slamming down on her clothes hamper. He had even heard the metal casters of her bed creaking against the wooden floor. But Myra had never cried out. Had she slept all night without discovering the corpse under her pillow?

Then again this morning he had waited for her to cry out when she fluffed up the pillow. But again there was no sound of protest. Myra was up and out early. That in itself was not too unusual. Maybe she had an early date with Warren—or whoever it was now.

His senses dulled, Jason lay in bed listening to the morning sounds. He could hear his mother panting as she heaved Gammer from the bed to the rocking chair. He could hear the strident tones of Gammer's TV. He could hear the sound of a car. Was it Myra leaving? Or was it his father driving down to the mailbox for the Sunday paper?

When he could stand it no longer, he pulled on a pair of cut-off jeans and a tee-shirt. Downstairs, it was like any other Sunday morning, except quieter.

His mother looked up when he slouched into the dining room. "There's frost this morning . . . on the garden. The pumpkin vines will go. Don't know why I always try with the pumpkins. . . . Oh, have you seen Gammer? She's much improved. . . ." Yes, his mother had things to say about the weather, about Gammer, and about the garden. Jason winced as he remembered. His mother's rambling conversation was not that different from what he had overheard at the Slavin's the night before.

His father was unusually silent and subdued. On Karl Hurd's face was the same quizzical expression he had worn the day before.

For breakfast there was only cold cereal. Myra was not around to whip up pancakes. Jason hadn't eaten in twenty-four hours, but the shredded wheat tasted like straw in his mouth. He had to choke it down with gulps of milk. He noticed that the barbells were inside this morning. It must have been too cool for Karl to work out on the front porch. But Nimbus was outside. Jason could hear him grunting and yelping viciously as though he'd just cornered some mole.

Jason got up from the table and wandered out of the house. He avoided looking at the dog as he made his way to the barn. It sounded as though Nimbus had finally caught something, and whatever it was, Jason didn't want to see it.

Feeling empty and dull, the cereal a tumbling lump in his stomach, he pulled himself up into the loft. He lay down in the hay and stared up at the roof with its endless knotholes. Absently, he reached out for Templeton's cage.

Without looking over, he sprung the latch and let the door fall open. His body braced for the bony little feet to run up over his chest. He expected the rough tongue to lick cereal crumbs from his fingers. But nothing happened.

Slowly, Jason rolled over. "Templeton, where are you? Are you hiding from me?" He listened, but there was no sound of scampering feet. Suddenly nervous, he rummaged through the loft, poking into every dim corner. No Templeton.

Jason held very still, not even breathing. Then, with slow, agonizing recognition, he exhaled. Now it all made sense. Myra silent. Myra gone. Templeton missing. Nimbus growling. Since when had Nimbus become a hunter? Since never.

Jason threw himself down from the loft and ran toward the porch where Nimbus was still snarling. He was screaming, and the dog retreated from him, trying to inch backward under the edge of the porch. But Jason could see the bloody thing in Nimbus' mouth—with its traces of black and white. That limp, bleeding pulp was Templeton. Or what was left of him.

Jason felt hot, cold, tense, shaky. A voice was shrieking, and he supposed it was his, but no sounds came out that made any sense to him. It was just wild, hysterical screaming.

His father was there and so was Myra. And Ellen Hurd? Was she there, too? Was she really telling him to quiet down—not to disturb Gammer?

Jason grabbed his father's walking stick from the porch. He was beyond all rational thought. Something had snapped. And it wasn't even Templeton really. A rat, Templeton was just a rat. Had been a rat and was a nothing now.

Everyone was making loud noises at him, but because he swung the walking stick they kept their distance. For a moment, Jason even thought Gammer was there, staring vacantly, and carrying the TV set locked in her bony arms.

He backed away from them. He wasn't screaming now, just backing up, fending off the dog with the stick. Then, abruptly, he stumbled against the car. That was it. He'd lock himself and his dead pet into the car. He fumbled for the handle. Then, dropping the walking stick, he opened the door and fell back into the front seat. His head was throbbing as he reached out to slam the door.

Numbly, he looked at the dashboard. The keys were dangling there. Without pausing to think, he switched on the ignition and started the car. He'd just drive away and never return. He'd crash the car. Or else, like Stuart Little, he'd just keep driving north. Swallowing down his own hysteria, he jerked the drive shaft into reverse.

He saw it all in the rear view mirror, but, somehow, looking in the mirror was like looking at a color TV set. It was all so remote and distant. The fender flying backward out of the barn was heading for a yelping gray dog. There was a thud. Jason pulled frantically at the gears. A small point of awareness told him he must stop the car, must reverse his direction. With a grinding of gears, the car lurched forward again—up and over something. Then it screeched into the front of the barn. Jason snatched the keys from the ignition and jumped from the car.

He knew without looking down. He saw the horror in all of their faces. He had hit Nimbus. Twice. He knelt down by the dog. He could see the tire print running across the grayish abdomen. There was no blood, but the dog's sides were heaving painfully. He was breathing, but his front legs were bent and flattened in a grotesque manner. Jason felt a surge of pity for the suffering animal. "I didn't mean to do it," he sobbed. His whole body shook, but there were no tears. "It was an accident. I didn't mean to." Horror-stricken, he looked up at his father, his mother, and his sister. They were all standing there in silence. Then, his father bent down. With cool, professional hands, Karl Hurd examined the legs, palpated the abdomen of the schnauzer. His face was grim.

He didn't say anything to Jason, but after a moment he rose and loped off toward the house. When he reappeared, he was holding the .22 rifle. With a touch that was unusually gentle, he pulled Jason to his feet. "You must," he said. "You must put an end to his misery."

"You do it," Jason whispered.

"No, Jason. You began it. You must end it."

Jason allowed himself to breathe in and out several times. Then, at last, he reached for the rifle. "How?" he asked.

"In the head," his father said, his voice cracking slightly. "Between the eyes. Put the barrel there and squeeze the trigger."

Jason looked down at the dog. He was panting now and writhing. A small pool of dark blood was running from his mouth.

He placed the barrel of the gun against the dog's head and carefully pulled the trigger. The shot was muffled. There was no other sound. A hole appeared in the animal's head. The body lay still except for some involuntary twitching.

Jason dropped the gun and bolted off into the woods. He knew just where he was going: the quarry. The quarry was waiting for him this morning—cold, clear, and bottomless.

I dare you, Jason. Dare you dare you dare you.

Somewhere inside his head, he heard the echo of Myra's voice. He didn't need her taunts today. Today it would be easy.

With slow, deliberate steps, he advanced toward the edge. He reached out and grabbed the swinging tire. He knew he'd jump, but something was nagging at him. Roseanne and Buddy. Maybe he should try and say good-by to them.

He backed up a few steps. Then a few more. Finally he turned toward Hawthorne. Somehow, he'd manage to avoid Sam and say a word to Roseanne. Take one more look at Buddy.

It didn't work out that way. Sam Slavin was waiting in the orchard—solemn and stiff-shouldered. He was picking up rotted fruit from under the trees. Jason began to back away. Everything was all wrong today.

"Stop," Sam called out. "I know about the dog. Your father phoned me."

"He always calls you, doesn't he?"

"Only when he thinks I can help. He called today because he thought you'd come here, and he wants you back. I don't agree with your father, Jason, but he *is* your father. And he wants you home."

"Did he tell you about the gun? That I had to shoot Nimbus?"

"Yes, he told me, and I'm sorry, Jason. But you can't stay here. He wants to talk to you. It would be wrong of me to let you hide out here."

Jason laughed bitterly. He had hidden there all summer. It was all right then, but not now. He advanced a few feet. Maybe he'd run for it, try to spurt past Sam to see Roseanne and Buddy.

"Stop," Sam said.

"Oh, shut up. I didn't come to see *you*. I came to see *them!*"

"No," Sam insisted, planting himself firmly in front of Jason. "Settle up with your father first and then we'll talk. I'm sorry I got mad at you on Wednesday. It was too much all at once. Buddy . . . and realizing it had been wrong to let you become so dependent on Roseanne and me. . . . Go on, Jason. Face up to your father. Be a man about it."

Be a man about it. Almost the very words his

father might have used. Well, he didn't want to be a man. Ever. "I hate you," Jason cried. "I hate you, *sir!*"

Sam bent down and began to scoop up handfuls of the soft, over-ripe plums. "Grow up, Jason," he muttered, struggling to control his temper. "Grow up!"

That did it. Jason turned and fled. He raced back to the edge of the quarry. This time he didn't bother with the tire and the rope. Numbly, he hurled himself off the edge. In a minute, he told himself, everything would be over.

But, in a minute he felt as though he were flying. Suddenly he was free of that awful, dragging weight. Instead of feeling full of hate and dull anger, he was alert and calm. He was soaring. His thin body made an arc above the water. With the wind blowing and the sun shining, the surface looked like wrinkled aluminum foil. Maybe it would rattle when he hit.

But there was no rattling sound, just a loud splash. And, cleanly, feet first, Jason sank into the water. Now he was spread out, flying under the surface. For an instant, he couldn't tell whether the water was burning hot or icy cold.

Then he felt the coldness and realized that this was a mistake. All of it. Jason Hurd was not going to sink and die. Despite Nimbus, Templeton, his father, Myra, Sam—Jason Hurd was not going to the bottom of the quarry. He just couldn't.

The pressure against his chest was increasing, and the weight of his clothes was pulling him down. His eyes open under the water, he watched the bubbles from his own mouth racing to the surface. Then, with perfect clarity, almost as though he'd taken an hour to work it out, he saw it all. He must follow those bubbles right up into the blue morning air. His lungs, like two pink balloons, would help lift him.

Pushing and flailing, he beat against the oppressive water with his fists. He got one good gulp of air before he was sucked under again. The water was strong, relentless as it pulled at him. If he relaxed for a moment, he felt weak and sluggish. His clothes dragged him down. But when he struggled, he felt strong and buoyant. He wouldn't sink down or die. He would keep fighting, pushing down against the water until he broke through its surface again.

When he gasped for air, it felt sharp and cold, prickling in his aching lungs. He looked around. Minor details seemed vivid and important. There was a fresh, musky smell to the air. He saw a yellow dragonfly skimming along the water. He saw the wooden frame of a house going up beyond the rim of the quarry. And he noticed that his watch was still on. He wondered if he should have taken it off before he jumped. Then the water drew him down again.

He was choking. There was pain in his ears, in his nose. But he had seen that sharp, beautiful world above the water, and he was determined to fight his way back up to it. At the surface he took another gulp of air. Maybe someone would appear now. Maybe Sam had followed him. Or his father or Myra.

But no one was there. It was all up to him. He had to do it alone. He had to *try*.

Like a baby first crawling, Jason moved his arms and legs, gradually pulling himself closer to the quarry wall. Waves kept slapping against his face. Water forced its way into his mouth and down his throat. He coughed. He sneezed. He was panting rapidly in an effort to keep his lungs filled with air.

In a minute he would be able to touch the limestone wall. As he reached out to take hold of a ledge, the water closed over him again. But he struggled, and he kept struggling until his fingers grasped the stone.

At last he was able to pull himself up out of the water and sprawl across the ledge. He didn't want to move. But, resisting the urge to lie there and savor the fact that he had saved himself, he got to his feet and climbed up the cliff. Then, warm despite the unseasonable chill of the day, Jason entered the woods, heading along the path to the Hurd farm.

The morning was beautiful. Small wet sparks shot out from the spider webs strung between low-hanging bushes. The leaves of the sumac where his clumsy tree house was perched were tinged with red.

A dry leaf crunched under his feet.

The leaf was dead. Nimbus was dead. Templeton

was dead. Those were facts he couldn't change. He could grieve and feel sorry for his own part in it. But death was always final. And Jason was not yet ready for such finality.

"I'm sorry, sir," Jason said. "It was an accident. I didn't like the dog, but I didn't mean to hurt him."

"I know that, son." Karl Hurd's voice wasn't tender, nor was it harsh. He pointed at Jason's clothes. "How did you get all wet?"

Jason didn't answer. He was staring at an old Army blanket with something bulging under it. Involuntarily, he shuddered. "I've come to bury the dog," he announced. "I'll go to Slavin's—use the power saw and make a box to put him in. I'm not much of a carpenter, but I think I can do that." He turned away.

"Wait," his father called after him. "Myra told me about your rat—how she let him go. I never liked that creature. Never could stand his feet. But, still, Myra was wrong. And I can understand your anger."

Jason paused, balancing his weight on one foot. Myra

was always right. She never admitted anything she had done wrong. "Did she tell you about the rabbit?"

"What rabbit?"

Jason winced. "The dead one from yesterday. The one she shot. I put it in her bed . . . to punish her for killing it."

"No, no, she didn't tell me."

So for once Myra hadn't tried to blame him. Well, maybe it was hard being Myra, too. Still, it would be a long time before he could forget the fact that she had taken Templeton out of his cage.

"Where is she?" he asked.

"Riding," Karl said absent-mindedly. He squinted at Jason. "You know, you never answered me about how you got wet."

"I—I was at the quarry," Jason said warily.

"At the quarry? Doing what? Swimming?"

Jason wasn't about to spill everything. Some things were private. "Well," he said, "sort of."

Karl Hurd cleared his throat. "Say, Jason, I'll help you bury the dog. You don't really need a box, you know."

Maybe not, but he didn't like the idea of shoveling dirt over the schnauzer's inert body. A box would be better. And more appropriate. Jason shook his head. "No, I can bury him myself, and I do want to fix up a box for him."

With the wet clothes still chafing his skin, he turned away and headed for Hawthorne. He didn't bother to plan out what he'd say. Something would come to him.

When he got there, he found that the station wagon was not in the driveway. The place was empty. Jason was glad. He really wanted to attend to the dog first. Then he'd come back and see the Slavins. First things first. One step at a time.

Hurriedly, he flipped on the saw. He selected two unused sheets of plywood and drew a few hasty lines. Then he severed the planks to make three sides, two ends, and a lid. Four feet by three feet by two feet. That should be big enough.

With rapid, clumsy strokes, he hammered the make-shift coffin together. The corners overlapped at one end. In another place the boards didn't quite meet. But that was all right. It didn't have to be perfect.

The whole procedure couldn't have taken more than twenty minutes. Then, with mounting impatience, Jason loaded the box onto the little go-cart Sam had made for Buddy. The lid was not attached to the box. He'd nail that down at home. Propping the lid in the box, Jason threw in a hammer and a bunch of nails and began pulling the go-cart down the trail toward the Hurd farm.

When he got back to the farm, he attended to the grisly job of getting the dead dog into the box. It wasn't easy. Rigor mortis had set in and the limbs were difficult to fit into place. But he finally did it— blanket and all. He couldn't bear to uncover the corpse.

He was about to nail on the lid when he remembered something else. Templeton. Taking a rag from the kitchen, Jason went to find the dead rat. Then he put it into the box with the dog.

With a choppy left-handed stroke, Jason began to nail down the lid. It didn't quite fit, but that was all right. He was somewhat nervous, knowing that his father was sitting on the front porch swing, watching him. Accidentally he hit his right thumb. Flushing with embarrassment, he stole a look at his father. Karl didn't seem to have noticed.

Jason's thumb throbbed, but he didn't mind. There would have been no pain at the bottom of the quarry. Just nothing. Nimbus was nothing. Templeton was nothing. But Jason—well, he was still something.

As soon as the box was nailed closed, Karl Hurd rose from the swing. "Now let me help you dig the hole, son."

Stubbornly, Jason shook his head. He'd do this himself. It was his fault the dog was dead, and he must attend to everything.

He dragged the box beyond his mother's vegetable garden to a plowed area where it would not be too hard to dig. Then he went back for a shovel. At first the work was slow and laborious, but with practice he learned to use the shovel in a more efficient way. Soon he was heaving up clods of dirt with mechanical precision. But his shoulders were aching, and the hole was not nearly big enough. Burying a large dog in a large box was not like burying a squirrel.

He decided to rest for a moment. Walking through the garden to the tomato vines, he picked off a plump, red tomato and bit into it. Juice and tiny seeds sprayed from his mouth. It tasted good. He lingered over it, reluctant to return to his digging.

When he had finished off the last bite, he went back to work. He tried to imitate the smooth rhythm he'd had a few minutes before, but he couldn't quite get it. He was tired.

Karl Hurd must have noticed that Jason was floundering. He came up behind his son carrying a second shovel. "Jason, I'd like to help," he said. Still, Jason refused. This was his job and he'd do it.

Despite the coolness, he was perspiring. When he licked at his lips, he tasted a bitter saltiness at the corners of his mouth. It was getting harder and harder to lift the shovel. Then, at last, he saw how stubborn he was being. It was too much, too big a job. He needed help.

Karl Hurd was leaning on the second shovel and staring down into the hole.

"Please, sir," Jason said. "I think I do need some help."

Together, Karl and Jason gouged out the hole. Together they lowered the box and covered it up. Then Jason threw down the shovel.

"Dad," he said slowly, "I don't know if this is the right time or the right thing to say—but I do want to board at Hawthorne this year. I hope you'll say yes."

For a moment Karl Hurd looked down at his son in silence. Then he shook his head. "No, Jason, I don't think so. At least not this fall. And it's not the money either. It's your attitude. Running away never solved any problems."

Jason stared at him. A minute ago, he had thought things might be different between them. Now he saw that is was all still the same. Well, almost the same.

". . . and I explained it all to Slavin when he called on Thursday to . . ."

"On Thursday?" Jason interrupted. "He called on Thursday?"

"Yes, he wanted to talk with you. He called after dinner, but you were off in the barn some place. So I just told him I knew you'd call when you were ready to talk. . . ."

"But why didn't you *tell* me?"

"I don't know, son. I didn't think it was that important. And, well, I just figured it was your place to call him and apologize."

Jason struggled to contain the old feelings of anger that were welling up in him. At least Sam had called last week. That made a difference. A big one. And maybe his father was right about Hawthorne. Maybe he *could* manage to get by at home. Maybe the Slavins wouldn't want him around all the time anyway.

When Jason spoke, the words came out calmly. "I think, sir, if you don't mind, I'll go over to Hawthorne and talk to Mr. Slavin. I think I should apologize. . . ."

"That's a good idea. Why don't you do that, son? But we'll be looking for you about lunch time."

Another day, Jason would have turned toward the woods and run all the way to Hawthorne. But he didn't. Instead, he headed toward the house. His talk with Sam Slavin could wait.

He put the two shovels away. Then he went to his room and stripped off his damp, muddy clothes. He turned on the shower and stepped in. It felt good to have the hot water beating down on his back. He took hold of the soap and wash cloth. With care, he washed off his arms and legs, washing off the quarry, washing off Nimbus and Templeton. Tall and thin he stood there watching the needles of water bounce off his skin. At last, he shut off the faucet and stepped out. As soon as he had dried off, he put on clean clothes and ran a comb through his hair.

Just as he was about to leave, he remembered Myra. Feeling very magnanimous, he wrote her a note in a quick backhand script. "I'm sorry about the rabbit," it said. For a signature, he scribbled the letter J. He placed the note in the arms of her purple octopus. Then, changing his mind, he reached out, crunched up the note and tossed it into Myra's wastebasket. Maybe she'd find it there, and maybe she wouldn't. He wasn't quite ready to forgive her.

As he turned back into the hall, he ran into his mother coming out of Gammer's room. "Oh, Jay, there are a few tomatoes. . . . I'd go pick them myself . . . but Gammer seems so restless."

Jason nodded and gave her a reassuring pat on the arm. "Sure, later," he promised, "after I get back from Slavins'."

Then he ran off toward Hawthorne. The station wagon wasn't back yet. He had been hoping he'd be able to get his apologies over quickly. Well, he'd just have to wait. He sat down on the front steps of the cottage.

At last, the dusty car rattled into the driveway. Jason sprang to his feet and watched Sam and Roseanne and Buddy get out. Somehow they all looked different. He saw a tall man with wild, reddish hair, a rounded blond woman who swayed from side to side as she walked, and a pale, staring child. He liked them. He was glad to see them. But now they were just his neighbors—his English teacher, his teacher's wife, and their nephew.

After a minute, Jason found his voice. "I borrowed some plywood for a coffin for the dog," he explained. "Then I went home and I buried—I mean, my father and I—buried him. And, well, now I'm here to tell you I'm sorry for what I said. Sorry for what I did to Buddy. I just tried to make things happen too fast. Is he all right?"

Buddy was standing there staring at him, not smiling or moving. Jason waved at the child. "Hi there, Buddy," he called, mustering a smile. Maybe Sam and Roseanne were just neighbors, but Buddy was still something special. And the Slavins hadn't sent him away yet.

Suddenly Buddy lurched forward. "Rum, rum, rum, rum," he cried hoarsely. With furious force, the child butted his head into Jason's stomach, sending them both sprawling into the driveway.

Jason could hear Roseanne's soft laugh. Sam knelt down in the driveway between the two boys. "Jason," he said, "we've just been in the city having a visit with Mrs. Homans. We've made up our minds about Buddy. He'll live at school this year. . . ."

"At school?"

"That's right, but he'll be spending all his weekends with us. Roseanne and I feel we mustn't try to keep him here with us full-time, and this was the best thing we could work out. *Now* the problem is to teach Buddy the days of the week. If he can learn them, he won't feel abandoned from Monday to Friday, Mrs. Homans says."

Sam lifted Buddy up to his feet and began brushing him off. "Maybe, Jason, you could help. Maybe if you're not too busy you'd help teach him that. If anyone can teach him, I guess it would be you. . . ."

Jason stood up. "Sure," he agreed. "I'll try to teach

Buddy the days. Do you think he can really learn them?"

Sam smiled and shrugged. "Beats me! I don't think I could teach him. But you ought to be able to find a way. He doesn't have to *say* them—just understand them."

"Well, I'll try," Jason said. If he could pull himself from the quarry, he could teach Buddy the days of the week, couldn't he? Lifting Buddy off the ground, he swung him around. "Monday, Tuesday, Wednesday," he chanted. "Or should I have started with Sunday?" He put the child down. "Listen, Buddy, you must learn: Sunday, Monday, Tuesday, Wednesday, Thursday, Friday, Saturday!"

"No," Buddy said, spinning himself around in a lopsided circle. "No, no, no, no, no."

Jason laughed. He was already going too fast. One step at a time. "All right," he said slowly, "this is Sunday. Let's start there. Maybe if I make you a wooden box with seven colored stones. Two yellow and five blue . . ."

"Wait a moment there," Roseanne interrupted. "We haven't had our lunch yet. Will you join us?"

Jason shifted his weight from one foot to the other. He liked the Slavins, and it would be a nice lunch. He hadn't had lunch with them in almost a week. He glanced over at Buddy. The boy was tracing dusty patterns on the fender of the station wagon. Already, he seemed to have forgotten that Jason was back.

Yes, it would be a nice lunch, but Jason wasn't sure he wanted to stay.

He looked down at his watch. Despite the quarry, it was still running. It was after twelve already. "I didn't know it was so late," he said. "I'd like to stay, but I don't think I should. My mother wanted me to pick some tomatoes. And . . . my father might be looking for me. Another day. All right?"

Jason looked over toward Buddy again. "Good-by, Buddy. See you later." Buddy didn't answer, but Jason smiled and waved at him anyway. Turning back to Sam and Roseanne, he said, "I'll be back this afternoon or tomorrow—as soon as I figure out a way to teach Buddy. Well . . . I'll see you. . . ."

Then, with a determined nod, he headed back toward his own house.

Susan Terris received her B.A. degree at Wellesley College and her M.A. degree in English literature at San Francisco State College. She is the author of many articles and short stories for children. She has also written several books, including *On Fire, The Upstairs Witch and the Downstairs Witch*, and *The Backwards Boots*.

Mrs. Terris and her husband David, a stockbroker, live in San Francisco with their three children—Danny, Michael, and Amy. Mrs. Terris was born in St. Louis and lived there until she was twenty. She has chosen the St. Louis area as the setting for THE DROWNING BOY. This book reflects her interest in wildlife and nature, which was first developed while she was growing up in Missouri. Today, Mrs. Terris pursues this same interest as she hikes with her family in California.